Heart of Mystic Valley

Montana Becketts ♦ Wild Spirit Ranch, Book Two

Historical Western Romance

SHIRLEEN DAVIES

Book Series by Shirleen Davies

<u>Historical Western Romances</u>
Redemption Mountain
MacLarens of Fire Mountain Historical
MacLarens of Boundary Mountain
Montana Becketts ♦ Wild Spirit Ranch

<u>Contemporary Western Romance</u>
Cowboys of Whistle Rock Ranch
MacLarens of Fire Mountain Contemporary
Macklins of Whiskey Bend

<u>Romantic Suspense</u>
Eternal Brethren Military Romantic Suspense
Peregrine Bay Romantic Suspense

Find all my books at:
https://shirleendavies.com/books/
The best way to stay in touch is to subscribe to my newsletter. Go to my Website,
www.shirleendavies.com, and fill in your email and name in the
Join My Newsletter boxes.
That's it!

Heart of Mystic Valley is a work of fiction. Names, characters, places, and incidents are either products of the author's imagination or used fictitiously. Any resemblance to actual events,

Cover design by Sweet 'n Spicy Designs
ISBN: 978-1-964063-31-7

I care about quality, so if you find something in error, please contact me via email at
shirleen@shirleendavies.com

Description

She's a feisty and tenacious newspaper editor.
He's a hardworking rancher and talented peacemaker.
Will their lifelong friendship survive the growing divide between them?

Faith Goodell is a formidable young woman. Following in her father's footsteps, she runs the Mystic Gazette newspaper on the principles of providing timely and accurate information to her readers. Though tired of lonely nights in her large home, she has little time for anything outside of being the paper's sole reporter, editor, and publisher. If it weren't for her best friend, Joshua, she'd have no social life at all.

Joshua Beckett takes satisfaction in hard work and long hours on his family's Wild Spirit Ranch. He spends little time wondering about his single life and if or when he'll meet the right woman and marry. Instead, he enjoys the company of his lifelong friend, Faith, applauding her determination to continue the good work her father started.

What causes concern is Faith's idea to form a Women's Alliance. While she views it as an expeditious way for women to have their voices heard, Joshua worries the group will cause a fraction in the community, impacting sales of the newspaper.

Adding to his worry are the threats of a roving gang of bank robbers who seem to have targeted the town of Mystic, and Joshua's growing realization his feelings for Faith have grown beyond friendship.

More frightening is the knowledge he has no idea what to do about them.

Heart of Mystic Valley, Book Two in the Montana Becketts ♦ Wild Spirit Ranch historical western romance series, is a clean and wholesome full-length novel with an HEA and no cliffhanger.

Table of Contents

Heart of Mystic Valley

Chapter One

"Hold on, Gavin," Joshua Beckett shouted over the wind's howl. "We're almost there."

The sky above was a bruised purple, threatening an early winter storm as Joshua Beckett urged his horse faster. The rugged Montana terrain blurred into a brown and green smear, rocks and scrub brush flying past like the flung toys of an angry child. In his arms, twelve-year-old Gavin lay curled against Joshua's chest, his face ashen, his breathing shallow.

"Faster, faster," Joshua muttered, more to himself than to Gavin, in an attempt to urge his dapple-gray gelding on.

Every jolt and bounce of the horse was a dagger to Joshua's heart. He knew the pain Gavin must be in, recalling the broken bone he suffered when he was about the boy's age. It wasn't just the physical hurt gnawing at him. The fear in the boy's eyes, the same fear he'd seen in other orphans' faces knowing they were alone in the world, clawed at Joshua's heart.

Behind him, Annalee rode hard on her sorrel mare, her usually bright and mischievous eyes now clouded with worry. She was the heart of the Beckett family, always quick with a smile or a kind word, but today, her face was a mask of grim determination.

"Josh!" she called, her voice snatched away by the wind. "How is he?"

He glanced back, slowing enough to let her catch up. "Gavin's tough. He'll make it."

They didn't slow as they hit the outskirts of Mystic, the small town's dirt streets nearly empty, save for a few curious onlookers. Annalee bit her lip, her face tightening with each gallop.

Her mare skidded to a halt, almost colliding with Joshua's gelding as he dismounted with Gavin in his arms.

The bell above the door of Wainwright's Clinic jingled as Joshua burst inside. Warmth from the wood stove slapped his cold cheeks, and the sudden change in temperature made Gavin stir and whimper.

"Doc!" Joshua yelled. "We need help!"

Doctor Caleb Wainwright emerged from a back room, tying a clean, white apron around his waist. His dark eyes took in the scene with practiced calm. He motioned for Joshua to follow as he walked toward the examination table.

"What happened?" Wainwright asked, already assessing Gavin with a clinical detachment.

"Bucked off his horse. Arm's broken, and he's got a gash on his head," Joshua said, his breath coming in ragged bursts. He gently laid Gavin on the table, then stepped back, running a hand through his disheveled hair.

"Please, Doc," Joshua said, his voice cracking with desperation. "Do whatever you can for him."

Annalee burst through the door, her cheeks flushed from the cold and the rush. "I tied up the horses," she said, then froze as she saw Gavin on the table, unconscious. "Is he—"

"He's in shock," Wainwright interrupted, not unkindly. He worked with swift, sure movements, splinting Gavin's arm with the precision of a carpenter. Annalee moved to stand next to Joshua, her hands wringing together like a washwoman's.

The room was silent except for the crackle of the wood stove and the occasional rustle of doctor's tools. Annalee's eyes were wide, her mouth a thin line of suppressed emotion. Joshua put a hand on her shoulder, and she leaned into him.

Wainwright finished tying the last bandage and stepped back, wiping his forehead with the back of his hand. "He'll be all right," he said, his eyes meeting Joshua's with quiet reassurance.

"The three of us were up in Diamond Canyon, looking for strays," Joshua explained. "We thought it'd be an easy ride out and back."

Annalee sighed. "It was my idea to take Gavin along. He's been itching to do more around the ranch."

Wainwright listened as he cleaned his hands, his expression unreadable. "And the arm? Just a fall?"

"The cry of a mountain lion spooked his horse," Joshua said. "It bucked, and he went flying. We got him here as quick as we could."

Annalee's eyes filled with tears. "He was so scared. I thought—" She broke off, unable to finish the thought.

The doctor walked over to them, placing a hand on Annalee's shoulder. "It's not your fault," he said, his tone making clear he spoke from experience.

Joshua stepped out into a brisk wind, the threat of an early winter becoming more real. He took a deep breath, filling his lungs with the bracing chill, then let it out in a long, weary sigh. The boardwalk creaked beneath his boots as he paced, tugging up his collar to ward off the cold.

"Joshua," a familiar voice called. He turned to see Faith Goodell, her blonde hair peeking out from beneath a wool hat. She hurried toward him, concern etched on her delicate features. "I heard someone say you brought Gavin in. What happened?"

"He took a bad fall off his horse. Broke his arm."

Her hand flew to her mouth. "Is he going to be all right?"

"Doc says he'll be fine, just needs some time to heal." He rubbed his neck. "Annalee and I feel terrible. He's like family, you know."

"You've always looked after him. Your family looks after all the boys you've taken in."

"Yeah. He's one of us, as are all of them." He felt the weight of his words sink deep into his chest. "We've had Gavin for so long, it's like he's a Beckett now."

"Please let me know if there's anything I can do."

"Thanks, Faith."

She tilted her head, studying him. "Joshua, you know I care about all of you. The boys included."

His thoughts flickered to all the times she'd come to the ranch. They always spent a good deal of time talking. He liked those talks, the way she questioned everything, the way she listened.

"These boys," Joshua continued, shifting uncomfortably. "They come to us with nothing. No family, no prospects. We try to give them a place, teach them the work, send them to school."

"It's a lot to take on. I've always admired what your family does."

"We're doing our best to give them a future." He glanced back toward the clinic. "Sometimes, life can be pretty rough."

The door of the clinic swung open, and Annalee stepped out onto the boardwalk. "Josh, the doc wants to talk to you."

He started toward the door, then paused and looked back at Faith. "Thanks again."

He entered the clinic, leaving them on the boardwalk. Annalee regarded Faith with a curious tilt of her head. "So," she said, dragging out the word. "I see you and Josh talking a lot these days."

Faith shrugged, noncommittal. "We're friends."

"Friends," Annalee repeated, a sly smile creeping onto her lips. "That's nice."

The door opened, and Joshua reappeared. "Doc's

giving Gavin something for the pain."

As if on cue, a weak voice called from inside the clinic. "Joshua?"

They peeked through the doorway to see Gavin, pale and groggy, cradling his newly cast arm. "Does this mean I don't have to go to school for a while?"

Annalee laughed. "You're not getting out of your numbers that easy."

"He's a tough boy," Faith said. "He's going to be fine."

Annalee gave a slow shake of her head. "Gavin was in so much pain."

Faith's eyes flickered with understanding. "Accidents happen to all of us, Annie. It wasn't anyone's fault."

Joshua studied Faith. He knew her kind words to his sister meant more than Faith realized.

"Is Gavin staying here in town?" Faith asked.

Joshua shook his head. "We'll take him back to the ranch. Doc says he'll be fine, as long as he takes it easy for a bit."

He lingered, looking back at Faith, his mind a tangle of thoughts and unspoken words.

"Faith," Joshua said, causing Annalee to stop from entering the clinic. "Thanks. Your support means a lot right now."

Faith took a step toward him. "Just remember, you don't have to do everything alone."

Annalee glanced between Faith and Joshua, noting the unspoken connection, the subtle shift in their dynamic. She raised an eyebrow but said nothing.

"Come on," Joshua said to Annalee. "Let's get back to Gavin."

The warmth of the wood stove cut through their layers of clothing. Outside, a small crowd had begun to gather, drawn by the news of the accident.

Joshua glanced through the window, casting a look at the gathering crowd, his thoughts already miles away in the mountains where the accident occurred.

Inside the clinic, the tension returned, settling over Joshua and Annalee like an unwelcome guest. They took seats near the examination table where Gavin lay, his chest rising and falling in a drugged sleep.

Annalee broke the silence. "Do you remember when you broke your arm? It was after church, and you were trying to climb old man Johnson's white oak tree?"

Joshua smiled. "I cried like a baby. Gavin's handling this a lot better than I did."

"You were six," Annalee reminded him, a touch of fondness in her voice. "And Ma made everything better with a kiss and an apple pie. Who's going to kiss Gavin's broken arm and bake him a pie?"

"Ma will. The same as always."

Annalee leaned her head on Joshua's shoulder.

Doctor Wainwright returned from the office. He checked the bump on Gavin's head, adjusted the sling, and made a few notes. Joshua and Annalee watched in silence, their eyes tracking the doctor's every move.

He turned to them, his expression softening. "Gavin's stable now. The splint and cast will hold until the bone starts to knit. Make sure he doesn't use the arm for anything strenuous."

"We need to get him back to the ranch," Joshua said. "I'll get a wagon from Josiah."

"Take it slow and keep him propped up, he should be fine," Wainwright said. "No chores for a few days. And he'll need plenty of rest. The pain will be worse before it gets better."

Annalee bit her lip. "What about school? He and a couple other boys ride into town each day."

The doctor sighed, considering. "He can go, but only if he's up to it. I know Lilian schools them when the weather's bad. Perhaps she can take over for the first week. Afterward, he should be fine riding to school."

"That'll work. Thank you," Joshua said, his voice filled with genuine gratitude. "We owe you." He reached out to grasp the doctor's outstretched hand.

"We really appreciate everything you've done. You're always here when we need you," Annalee said.

Wainwright waved a hand dismissively, but a trace of a smile tugged at his lips. "It's my job. Just take good care of him."

"We will," Joshua promised. "He's in good hands."

They prepared to leave, bundling up in their coats and scarves. The warmth of the clinic had seeped into their bones, giving them a brief respite from the harsh wind waiting outside.

Annalee touched Joshua's arm. "I'll wait with Gavin. You tell Josiah at the livery to ready a wagon."

The siblings looked at each other, and he gave a reluctant nod.

By the time he returned with the wagon, Gavin was ready to get back to the ranch. Annalee helped Gavin into the back of the wagon, covering him with a blanket before climbing out to mount her horse.

Joshua tied his horse to the back of the wagon before climbing onto the seat.

Gavin's eyes fluttered open and he glanced around. "Where's my horse?"

"I took him to the livery. Josiah will take real good care of him until I can come back and get him."

"Okay."

"Just rest, Gav," Annalee said. "We'll get you back to the ranch in no time."

Joshua shifted to look back at him. "Remember when you first came to the ranch, scared and silent? Look at you now, causing all this ruckus."

Gavin tried to smile but drifted back into a restless slumber. Joshua glanced over his shoulder every few minutes to check on him. He was already considering who would pick up Gavin's chores for the next few weeks. The important matter was ensuring Gavin healed properly.

As if reading her brother's mind, Annalee reined her horse closer to the wagon. "We'll get through this. We always do."

Joshua nodded, knowing she was right. The Beckett family had faced numerous challenges over the years, and they'd met each one with the same resolve. This was just another hurdle, he told himself.

Chapter Two

Faith Goodell leaned across her cluttered desk, her gaze bright as she described her reasons for wanting to organize a women's group in Mystic.

"It's not just about women getting the vote, Maisy. We need a place where women can gather, support each other, and make our voices heard. Especially women business owners. The men have their say in everything. Why shouldn't we?"

Maisy Cox, her dark hair pinned up in a hurried twist, considered Faith's words. She was the quieter of the two sisters who ran the Golden Griddle, but her silence often carried more weight than a shout.

"You're right. Do you really think the women of Mystic are ready for a group like this? It's a big change. Bozeman has twice the number of women business owners as Mystic. We may not get the support you expect."

"We won't know until we try," Faith countered, a wry smile tugging at her lips. "Remember when your sister, Aggie, wanted to add ground elk meatloaf to the menu? Everyone thought it was madness. Who would order the meatloaf when they can get an elk instead? Now the meatloaf is one of the most popular dishes on your menu."

Maisy shrugged, conceding the point. "All right. So, what issues will we focus on first?"

Faith grabbed a pencil and started scribbling on a piece of newsprint. "Taxes, growing businesses, the right to vote, supporting the church's children's fund, and opening a library. Can you imagine how wonderful it would be to have a library in Mystic?"

Maisy peered over Faith's shoulder, her eyes thoughtful. "It sounds ambitious. Who will lead this group?"

"Initially, I will," Faith said, sitting back in her chair. "My idea is for it to be a collective effort. Every woman will have a chance to lead and to speak."

"You know Aggie and I are with you. But prepare yourself. Not everyone will be so supportive."

"I know." Faith sighed. "We have to start somewhere. Your backing means a lot."

Maisy stood and gathered her shawl. "I'm going to talk with Aggie. We'll see you soon. Good luck. We'll definitely need it."

Faith watched as Maisy walked out into the brisk autumn morning. Her determination was as unyielding as the Montana winter, and she knew the first step was simply spreading the word.

The clatter of the old printing press filled the room as Faith carefully fed paper into its maw. It had taken her two hours to set the type and wood blocks for the images. Each large sheet came out with bold, black letters proclaiming the formation of the Mystic Women's Alliance and details of their first meeting on Sunday after church.

When she finished, and the sheets were dry, Faith cut them into 11 X 14 posters. She stacked the papers and read one over, satisfaction washing over her.

An hour later, she was making her rounds through town, the chill air nipping at her cheeks. The Mystic community was tight-knit and sometimes resistant to change. She liked to think growing up here gave her an advantage. She understood the rhythms of the town, the way people swayed with new ideas before either embracing them or letting them fall away.

At Butterman's Boardinghouse, she handed a poster to Rosamund Butter, who accepted it with her usual warmth. "Maisy mentioned this to me. This is quite exciting, Faith."

Faith smiled. "As you can see, the first meeting is set for Sunday after church. I hope we get a good turnout."

"I only serve breakfast and supper on Sundays, so I'll be able to attend. I'm looking forward to hearing what others have to say," Rosamund said.

Next, she stopped at Jenning's Mercantile. The bell above the door tinkled as she entered. She waved to Casper Jennings, who stood behind the counter sorting bolts of fabric. His once-thick hair was now a sparse halo around his scalp, giving him an angelic appearance.

"Casper, how's business?" Faith called, walking up to the counter.

"Faith Goodell," he said, his voice carrying a note of fondness. "Busy as ever. What can I do for you?"

She held up a poster. "I was hoping you could mention this to your women customers. We're starting a group to discuss issues affecting us all."

Casper took the poster and adjusted his spectacles. He read it slowly, his lips moving with each word. "A women's alliance, eh? Sounds a little progressive."

"It's important we have a place to talk about issues that matter to us, Casper. Like taxes and education. You know how much I care about this town."

He scratched his chin, looking uncertain. "You know my Melody has strong opinions about these things. If I start pushing this, she might think—"

"Just mention it," Faith interrupted, her tone pleading but firm. "Let the women decide for themselves."

Casper set the poster down and removed his glasses, rubbing the bridge of his nose. "I'll see what I can do."

Deflated, Faith muttered her thanks and left the store. As she walked down the boardwalk, she thought about what Maisy had said. *Not everyone would be supportive.* Faith knew this, but Casper's hesitation stung more than she expected.

Back at the Gazette office, she fired up the printing press again and made a few tweaks to the original design. The new posters emphasized how the group would discuss various issues affecting Mystic, making it sound less like a radical movement and more like a community forum.

When the ink was dry, she headed back to Jenning's Mercantile. Casper looked surprised to see her again so soon.

"I made some changes." She handed him the new poster. "I think this better explains what we're trying to do."

Casper read it over and nodded, a small smile forming. "This looks more reasonable. All right, Faith, I'll mention it. No promises, but I'll mention it."

"That's all I ask. Thank you, Casper."

She left the mercantile with a lighter step, reminding herself even small victories could turn the tide.

Maisy slipped into a chair at the Golden Griddle, rubbing her hands together to chase away the cold. The restaurant was quiet, a lull between the breakfast rush and lunch crowd. Her sister, Aggie, stood behind the counter, flipping through a worn cookbook.

"How did it go?" Aggie asked, looking up.

"Faith is determined, as always," Maisy said. "She makes a convincing case. I think the group could really make a difference."

Aggie closed the cookbook and leaned on the counter, her gray eyes intent. "We've always supported her, you know that. But this is different. It's a bit more political."

Maisy shrugged. "Remember when folks got upset because we started serving coffee from a dealer in Seattle? They wanted what they knew, even if the new coffee was better. It didn't take long for them to appreciate the new beans. Sometimes, change is necessary."

Aggie considered her sister's words and nodded. "You're right. So, what can we do to help?"

"Faith needs a good turnout for the first meeting. We should go, of course, and maybe bring something to eat. Spice bread and the new pumpkin bread recipe you've been working on."

"Food always helps," Aggie said. "All right, we'll make a batch of each. Let's hope the other women are as willing as we are."

Meanwhile, Faith returned to the Gazette and sat at her desk, staring at the article about a new bull a local rancher had bought. She set it aside.

She'd been relieved when Casper agreed to mention the meeting but knew his willingness was only the beginning. The first meeting had to be a success if they were to gain any momentum.

She thought about the women in Mystic. All of them worked as hard as the men, yet had little say in matters affecting their lives. Would they see the value in what she was proposing? Would they risk the disapproval of their husbands and the community?

Standing, she moved to the old printing press and ran her fingers along its metal frame. It had been her father's, and working the press always made her feel closer to him. He'd taught her the power of the written word, the way a single article or pamphlet could spark a revolution.

She loaded a new roll of paper and let the machine take it, watching as the ink was applied with precise pressure. The press groaned and clanked as it came to life, a mechanical heartbeat that echoed her own growing anticipation.

With a stack of freshly printed posters in hand, Faith made her way to the mayor's office. Carl Jurgen had been mayor for as long as she could remember, balancing his public duties with running the town's lumberyard. He was a fixture in Mystic, his wiry frame and quick-talking nature well known to every resident.

The mayor's office was a modest affair, tucked above the lumberyard's storefront. Faith climbed the creaky wooden stairs and knocked on the paneled door. A muffled "Come in!" greeted her, and she pushed the door open to find Carl seated behind a cluttered desk, papers strewn about like fallen leaves.

"Faith Goodell! To what do I owe this pleasure?" Carl said, standing and extending a hand. Faith shook it, noting the rough calluses that spoke of a man unafraid to work alongside his employees.

"Mayor Jurgen, I'm here to ask for your support on something important." She took a seat opposite him and handed him a poster. Carl put on his reading glasses, peering at the paper with the intensity of a beekeeper inspecting a hive.

"A women's alliance? This is ambitious," he said, setting the poster down. "What's your aim with this, Faith?"

She took a deep breath. "We want to create a space where women can discuss issues that affect us all. Taxes, education, charitable works. It's not about stirring trouble. It's about making sure our voices are heard."

Carl leaned back in his chair, intertwining his fingers over his stomach. "You know I've always respected your family, Faith. Your father was a fair man, and you've followed in his footsteps. But this... some might see it as upsetting the balance."

"We're not looking to upset anything," she said, her voice unwavering. "We just want to contribute more directly to the community. Mayor, you know how hard the women in this town work. Isn't it only fair for us to have a say?"

Carl considered her for a long moment, his bird-like eyes unblinking. "What do you need from me?"

"Just your support. If you could mention the meeting during the town hall meeting tomorrow, it would mean a lot."

The mayor removed his glasses and rubbed his temples. "All right, Faith. I'll mention it. But remember, balance is key."

"I will. Thank you. We appreciate it."

As she stepped out into the crisp air, she allowed herself a small, hopeful smile.

The white steeple of the Mystic Church stood in stark contrast to the gray sky, a beacon of faith in the small community. Faith pushed open the heavy oak door and stepped inside, where warmth wrapped around her like a quilt. The church was empty, save for Pastor Owen Ward, who was arranging hymnals near the altar.

"Pastor Ward," Faith called softly, not wanting to disturb the serene atmosphere. Owen looked up, his ruddy face breaking into a warm smile.

"Faith, it's good to see you. How are you?" He walked to meet her in the center aisle.

"I'm well, thank you. I wanted to talk to you about something we're starting up," she said, handing him a poster. "It's a group for the women of Mystic. We'll be discussing issues that affect all of us, including ways to support the church's children's fund."

Owen read the poster, nodding slowly. "Sunday after church, huh?"

"Yes, Pastor."

"Well, I think this is a fine idea. The women of this town do so much already. The church women are always busy helping out parishioners and distributing Bibles. Giving them a platform to organize and speak out on other issues is only right."

Relief washed over Faith. "So, you'll support us? Maybe mention it to the congregation?"

"You have my support," Owen said. "And I'll make

sure Catherine spreads the word as well. The charitable aspects alone make it well worth the effort."

"Thank you, Pastor. This means a lot."

Owen placed a gentle hand on her shoulder. "Your father would be proud, Faith. Remember, every great change starts with a small, courageous step."

Faith left the church with a renewed sense of purpose. She envisioned a room full of women, all eager to make a difference.

Back at the Gazette, Faith hung up her coat and sat at her rolltop desk. The wood had worn smooth from years of use, and she liked to trace the grain with her fingers when she needed to think. Today, her thoughts came quickly, fueled by the tentative support she'd garnered from the mayor and the pastor.

She pulled a sheet of letterhead from a drawer and loaded it into her typewriter. For a moment, she stared at the contraption her father had purchased on a trip back east, not long after they became available. The Remington typewriter had a few flaws, but she loved the black machine. The clack of the keys filled the small office as she pounded out the headline.

"New Mystic Women's Alliance Seeks to Address Important Community Issues."

The article flowed from her fingertips, each sentence crafted with care. She explained the purpose of the group, the issues they planned to address, and the importance of women having a voice in the community. She detailed the first meeting, inviting all women of Mystic to come and share their thoughts.

Writing was where Faith felt most at home, where she could pour out her passion and reason in equal measure. As she neared the end of the article, she chose her words with extra caution, wanting to leave a lasting impression:

"We believe a stronger voice for women will lead to a stronger Mystic. Join us as we take the first steps toward a more unified community."

She imagined women reading the article over their husband's shoulders, feeling a spark of hope. Faith leaned back, wishing Joshua was here to give his opinion.

Chapter Three

Faith read the article through once more, making minor adjustments and savoring each word. Satisfied, she set it aside for the next edition of the Gazette. A wave of accomplishment washed over her, mingling with the anticipation of what was to come.

She stood and stretched, looking out the window. The town had changed so much since she was a girl, yet some things remained the same. Change was a slow beast, she knew, but it was not immovable.

Grabbing her coat, she headed for the door, posters in hand. With each step, she felt the weight of history pressing down while a lift of possibility pulled her forward.

Determined to talk to someone at every business, Faith continued along the boardwalk, stopping at key locations to tack up posters. The board outside the post office was a tangle of notices and advertisements. She found a space near the center and pinned up one of her posters as if it were a piece of art.

As she turned to leave, she nearly collided with

Mrs. Gloria Graham, a stern woman with a face carved from granite. Tall and slender, she had a regal bearing and had a tendency to look down on most of the townsfolk. Her husband was president of the Bank of Mystic, which Mrs. Graham believed put her above everyone else. She glanced at the poster and then at Faith.

"What's this about, Miss Goodell?" she asked, suspicion coloring her words.

Faith smiled. "We're starting a group for the women of Mystic to discuss town issues. We want to have a say in how the town is run. You should come to the first meeting. It will be held at my house after church on Sunday."

Mrs. Graham harrumphed, but Faith noticed she lingered to read the poster more closely as she walked away.

At the livery, she handed a poster to young Jeremiah Jarvis, who promised to give it to his father, Josiah. She posted another at the train depot, then made her way to the schoolhouse. The building was empty, the children having gone home for the day.

She opened the front door and peeked inside, finding a large chalkboard split into sections. One part listed arithmetic problems. Another had a cursive writing lesson. The final, smaller section held various announcements, and Faith was pleased to see one of her posters already up.

Closing the door quietly, she thought about Evelyn Graham. The teacher had been a steadfast friend, even during the difficult times when Faith's father died. Knowing she had friends like Evelyn, like the Beckett clan, gave her the strength to push forward.

Every conversation, every curious glance, built her resolve higher.

Faith paused at the end of the block. From here, she could see most of Mystic, including the church steeple, the schoolhouse, and the small cemetery on the hill. This was her home, and every building, every street, held memories for her.

She thought about the progress she'd made. The mayor would mention the meeting, the pastor had given his blessing, and even Casper Jennings had come around. It wasn't a groundswell of support, but it was a start.

The women of Mystic were strong, she knew. Many were like her, balancing work and family, trying to carve out a small piece of happiness. They didn't need saving. They needed their voices heard. Her group would provide a platform for their views, if only they were brave enough to seize it.

The bell on the Gazette's front door jingled, and Faith looked up from her desk. Maisy Cox walked in, followed closely by Evelyn Graham. Faith's face lit with genuine joy. These two women were more than allies. They were friends.

"Don't tell me you're here to dissuade me," Faith teased as they approached her desk.

"Quite the opposite," Evelyn said, shrugging off her coat. "We're here to help. Isn't that right, Maisy?"

Maisy nodded, though her eyes held a hint of reservation. "We want this to succeed as much as you do."

Faith stood and hugged them both in turn. "Thank you. I can use all the help I can get."

The three women set to work, cutting out handbills from larger sheets of newsprint and stacking them neatly. Faith had already made and passed out thirty, but she knew having extras wouldn't hurt. As they worked, they talked about the upcoming meeting and what they hoped to achieve.

"Do you really think the men will let us do this?" Evelyn asked, her tone more curious than doubtful.

"They don't have to let us," Faith said, her conviction unshakable. "We're not asking for permission. We're just doing what needs to be done."

"Still," Maisy said, "it helps that some of them are supportive. Like Casper Jennings."

"And Joshua Beckett," Evelyn added.

At the mention of Joshua Beckett, Faith's heart did a little flip. The Beckett family was large and influential, and having them on her side was crucial. It was Joshua's personal support she cherished most.

"Yes," she said, perhaps a bit too softly. "Joshua understands."

Finished with cutting the posters, they prepared an agenda for the first meeting and sat back, reviewing their work. Each woman held different thoughts and different anxieties. For now, they were united in purpose.

"This is going to be something special," Evelyn said, breaking the silence. "I can feel it."

Their excitement was contagious, and for a brief, shining moment, Faith believed everything would go exactly as planned.

With the handbills ready, Faith set out once more. This time, she planned to talk to one of the wealthiest men in Mystic.

She stopped in front of the Starlight Saloon. The large, two-story building was from Mystic's rougher days, its façade a mix of well-maintained weathered wood and white paint. Pushing through the swinging doors, Faith was greeted by the smell of beer, cigar smoke, and the low hum of afternoon patrons.

Doyle Shaw, the saloon's boisterous owner, spotted her immediately. "Faith Goodell! What brings the town's finest journalist to my humble establishment?" He waved her over. His dark hair and broad shoulders gave him an imposing presence, though his eyes always held a spark of mischievous friendliness.

"Doyle," Faith said, walking to the bar where he stood. "I'm here on official business." She handed him a poster, and Doyle set down his whiskey before taking it. He whistled low as he read.

"A women's alliance. Well, isn't that something? Planning to overthrow us menfolk, are you?" His tone was jesting, but Faith recognized the underlying tension.

"We're looking to contribute, not to overthrow," she said, meeting his gaze. "Can I count on you to post it somewhere visible?"

Doyle considered her for a moment, then nodded. "I'll put it by the door. Lots of the fellas talk when they're here. Their wives will hear about the meeting."

"Thank you," Faith said, turning to leave.

"Hold on a second," Doyle said, stopping her in her tracks. "I think what you're doing is a good thing. Women should have an equal say. My mother raised me to believe that."

Faith turned back, surprised. "Your mother was a wise woman. So, you'll support us?"

"I will," Doyle said, then hesitated. "In fact, I'd like to come to the first meeting."

Faith's eyebrows shot up. "You want to attend? Doyle, it's a women's group."

"I know," he said, leaning on the bar. "If you're serious about equality, shouldn't men be involved, too? A lot of the issues you'll be discussing affect us just as much. I think a male perspective could be useful."

Faith chewed on his words. He had a point, and having Doyle's support could lend the group legitimacy. Whether you liked or disliked Doyle Shaw, his support could deter any detractors. Still, it was a risky proposition.

"We need to create a space where women feel

comfortable speaking freely," she said. "Your presence might make some of them hold back."

Doyle shrugged. "It's your call. Just remember, we're all in this together. Whether you like it or not."

She thought hard, weighing the potential benefits against the possible backlash. "All right. You can attend the first meeting on Sunday. As an observer only, unless one of the women asks you a direct question. We'll see how it goes."

"Fair enough." Doyle extended a hand. Faith shook it, sealing their agreement.

As she stepped into the late afternoon sunlight, she wondered if allowing Doyle to attend was a stroke of genius or the beginning of trouble.

Faith nearly collided with Joshua Beckett as she hurried away from the saloon. The tall rancher caught her by the shoulders, steadying her before she could topple over.

"Joshua," she said, breathless. Her heart did its usual dance at the sight of him. His eyes searched hers with concern.

"Faith, are you all right? And what were you doing in the Starlight?" He glanced at the saloon's entrance. His tone carried the weight of an older brother scolding a sibling, and it set Faith on edge.

"I was talking to Doyle," she said, pulling a handbill from her bag and thrusting it at him. "About this."

Joshua took the flyer and read it, his expression shifting from curiosity to something more guarded. "A women's alliance. Does Annalee know about this?"

"Of course she does. Well, she knows I'm trying to organize a women's group. Josh, why do you sound so disapproving? This is important."

He sighed, shoving his hands in his coat pockets. "I don't disapprove, Faith. I just... I worry about you. About how this will be received."

"We can handle a little criticism," she said, crossing her arms. "We're not as fragile as you think."

"I never said you were fragile," he countered, his voice growing firmer. "But you could stir up a lot of things. People might take your meetings in the wrong way."

She bristled, uncrossing her arms and standing taller. "Take it the wrong way? We're just trying to have a say in our own lives, Joshua. Why is that so threatening?"

"It's not threatening," he said, exasperation creeping in. "But change like this doesn't happen overnight. You need to be prepared for—"

"For what? For the men of Mystic to tell us to sit back down and be quiet?" She shook her head, anger flaring in her eyes. "I thought you, of all people, would understand."

His face softened, and he reached out as if to touch her arm. "Faith, I'm just trying to—"

"To protect me? I don't need protecting, Joshua. I need your support."

She turned on her heel and started walking away. "Faith, wait," he called after her, but she didn't stop.

"I have work to do," she said over her shoulder, her pace quick and determined. "I'll see you later."

Faith left Joshua to stare after her, wondering what had just happened.

Chapter Four

Joshua Beckett rode toward home, letting his horse set the pace as he lost himself in thought. The autumn air carried a bite, hinting at the harsh winter to come. He pulled his collar up against the wind and considered the contentious discussion with Faith. Her sharp wit had been as constant as ever.

Their history was long. As children, they'd run wild along the riverbanks, more like siblings than friends. Joshua smiled, remembering the time she'd punched him square in the nose for mocking her new bonnet. He'd bled all over it, ruining the thing, and she'd cried. Her tears weren't for his injury. They were for the bonnet she'd so proudly worn to Wild Spirit Ranch from town. Even then, her passion had been something to reckon with.

Contrasts defined them. His calm against her tempestuous nature, his slow deliberation versus her rapid decisions. Yet those differences had forged a resilient friendship, one able to weather any storm. He wondered if their heated conversation in town would change anything.

The familiar sight of Wild Spirit Ranch came into view, its sprawling acres a testament to his family's enduring labor.

Memories surged like spring runoff in Joshua's mind. He saw them both as children again, barefoot and sunburned, two small figures cutting through tall grass and leaping over rocks.

One summer day, they'd constructed a makeshift raft from old timber and set out to conquer the river. Faith had stood at the bow like a pirate queen, daring the currents, while Joshua paddled with cautious strokes. When the raft hit a snag and splintered, dumping them into the icy water, it was Faith who'd laughed first, her fearless howl infectious. Joshua had joined in, even as he shivered and worried about explaining his soaked clothes to his mother.

Then there was the winter they'd gone trapping with Joshua's father and brothers. Faith had set her snares as his father had instructed, her eyes alight with the thrill of the hunt. Joshua, having done this for a few years, kept a close watch on her. When they found a rabbit caught and struggling, Joshua had freed it, letting it bolt into the snowy underbrush. Faith had protested at first, then relented, realizing the animal was too small to keep.

"You're too soft, Josh," she'd said, arms crossed. "It's survival—"

"Survival?" he'd cut in, hurt and defensive. "I'll survive just fine, Faith. I don't have to kill everything I see."

They hadn't spoken for a week, the longest silence in their friendship. It was Faith who'd broken it, sharing her school lunch and handing him a written apology. She'd never said the words "I'm sorry," but Joshua knew her well enough to read between the lines.

Their friendship had always walked a tightrope, balancing her unyielding nature with his more flexible spirit. Each clash and reconciliation only tightened the bond between them.

Joshua dismounted and led his horse to the barn, his mind still lingering in the past.

Warm light spilled from the Beckett homestead. Joshua hung his hat by the door, his stomach growling at the rich aroma of roasted meat. He hadn't realized how hungry he was until now.

The family was already assembled in the dining room, a large space dominated by an oak table handcrafted by Millard Beckett, their late patriarch. Around it sat three generations of Becketts. Matriarch Naomi, eldest son Grayson with his wife Jolene, and the various sons and daughters who made up the sprawling clan.

"Josh," called Jolene, her voice warm. "We thought you'd be staying in town."

"Just late," he said, taking an empty seat beside his mother.

Grayson raised a hand, and the room fell silent. "Lord, we thank you for this food, for our family, and for the strength to do our work. Amen."

"Amen," echoed the table, and the sound of utensils and voices filled the room.

"How's the new foal?" asked Annalee.

"Strong and spry," Cody answered. "A real beauty. We'll need a name soon."

"Call him 'Workload'," suggested Nathan, another brother, with a sly grin. "Seems fitting."

Laughter rippled around the table. Joshua noted how Nathan's eyes darted to Naomi, measuring her reaction. Of all the siblings, Nathan was the most prone to jest.

Naomi passed a dish of green beans to Gavin, her eyes softening and lips twitching.

Joshua ate slowly, savoring each bite, but more than that, he savored the company. He watched his family with the keen eye of a herdsman surveying his flock. This was his true gift. Always the peacemaker, he could sense the underlying currents and unspoken truths binding people together.

Grayson and Jolene were holding hands beneath the table, a subtle gesture of affection that spoke volumes about their union. In contrast, Cody sat slightly apart, his posture erect and his movements precise, as if conserving energy for a battle only he anticipated.

Gavin, usually full of chatter, was subdued tonight. His eyes tracked the conversation like a pup sidelined from play. Joshua knew the boy was suffering. A broken arm was bad enough, but the enforced idleness gnawed at Gavin's spirit.

Then there was Naomi. In her fifties, she was a force of pure energy, her wiry frame and sharp eyes undiminished by age. Yet tonight, Joshua thought he detected a weariness in her, a rounding of the shoulders suggesting more than simple fatigue.

"First snow can't be far off," Grayson said, breaking into Joshua's thoughts. "We need to get a move on with winter preparations."

A murmur of agreement went around the table. The changing seasons dictated the rhythm of their lives, and everyone understood what was coming.

"We still have the last cutting of hay to finish," said Cody, the second oldest. "Weather holds, we can knock it out in a couple of days."

"Calves need weaning," added Parker, the youngest Beckett brother.

Grayson nodded. "We'll split the crews, mixing the older hands with the boys. They don't have school tomorrow. Cody, you take the ranch hands for the hay. Parker and I will handle the calves."

"What about the barns?" Annalee interjected. "Roofs are still leaking, and the south wall of the big shed is about to give."

"I can take the barns," said Joshua. "The boys need the practice. We'll shore things up."

"Firewood's low," Nathan said. "I'll tackle it after checking the fences." Everyone knew there weren't many, mostly the corrals and around the homestead.

All eyes turned to Naomi, who weighed the plans with the authority of a judge deliberating a verdict. "That leaves the garden," she said. "We'll need all the vegetables in, and the beds turned over." She looked to the women, who nodded. "We can manage."

The division of labor settled, everyone relaxed. This was how the Becketts worked, with each person knowing their role.

"We should put Gavin to work," Joshua said, casting a look at the quiet boy.

"He could help me stack wood with his good hand," Nathan offered. "And feed the chickens."

"He needs to heal," Naomi said, her tone brooking no argument. "There's plenty of time for work."

The table fell quiet for a moment, the only sound the clink of silverware on porcelain. Joshua knew Nathan would offer Gavin something to do instead of sitting around the bunkhouse.

Annabell stood. "How about dessert?"

The sun rose hesitantly, veiled in a thin layer of clouds that smeared the sky with pastel hues. Frozen dew sparkled on the grass, quickly disappearing as the Becketts set about their work.

In the north pasture, Grayson and Parker moved among the herd, separating cows from their calves with practiced ease. The air was filled with the plaintive cries of the young cattle, a chorus of protest against their enforced independence.

Down in the lower fields, Cody, two older ranch hands, and a couple of the younger boys worked in unison, their scythes rising and falling like the pistons of a great engine. They shouted and laughed, their camaraderie palpable as they made short work of the last standing hay.

At the main compound, Joshua stood atop a ladder, surveying the roof of the big barn. He had a hammer in one hand and a roll of tar paper in the other.

"Need more nails up here," he called down to Little Joe, one of the boys. "And be quick about it."

The lad sprinted off. Joshua slid the hammer into his work belt and took a moment to stretch his back. The view from the roof was expansive, giving him a brief sense of mastery over the land. He spotted Nathan fifty yards away near the tree line, wielding an axe with measured strokes. A growing pile of split logs testified to his morning's labor.

Nathan paused to wipe his brow, then looked over the growing pile of wood. Joshua knew he'd be coming back for the wagon before lunch to transport the firewood to spots near the house and bunkhouse.

He glanced over at Joshua, who was directing two young boys on how to replace a rotted door. Joshua caught his brother's look and shrugged, causing Nathan to laugh.

In the garden behind the house, the women worked with swift, sure hands. The earth was cold and resistant, but they dug and pulled with the tenacity of miners extracting the last vein of ore. Carrots, potatoes, and turnips filled their baskets, dirt clinging to the vegetables like unwilling tenants.

Jolene stood and stretched. "That's the last of it," she announced, wiping a strand of hair from her face.

"Thought we'd never get done."

"We're not done yet," said Naomi, ever the task-master. "Still need to blanch and jar these."

Annalee and Lilian, the youngest of the Beckett sisters, exchanged weary glances. At twenty-three and nineteen, both were full of restless energy, though for different reasons. Annalee wanted to be out with the men, and Lilian wished she were curled up in her room, reading the book she'd borrowed from Joshua.

The women moved inside, where the heat of the wood stove created a welcome contrast to the crisp outdoor air. They peeled and chopped, their motions rhythmic and hypnotic. Steam rose from pots, filling the kitchen with a savory haze.

Little Cody, Jolene and Grayson's infant son, lay on a quilt in the corner. He alternated between watching his mother work and kicking his legs into the air. His cheeks were flushed, whether from the heat or a budding fever, no one could yet tell.

The day wore on, each hour a testament to the Becketts' enduring work ethic. In the pastures, Grayson, Parker, and ranch hands finished their weaning, the calves now corralled and the mothers grazing quietly. They rode back to the main compound, their silhouettes merging with the landscape.

Cody and his crew had stacked the hay high, creating towering walls of fodder that would see the livestock through the winter. Their shirts were soaked with sweat, their faces bronzed from the intensity.

Nathan had cut and stacked more wood than

they'd need, his hands raw and blistered from years of calluses. He hauled his axe and tools back to the shed, his gait indicating his exhaustion.

At the barns, Joshua and his group had patched roofs and reinforced walls, their handiwork solid and dependable. The young ranch hands had gained valuable experience, and Joshua was pleased with their progress.

Inside the house, the women had finished preserving the vegetables. Rows of mason jars lined the counters, their contents a rainbow of sustenance. Naomi and the girls took a moment to admire their work before dispersing to tend to other duties.

Joshua looked to the horizon, gauging the time by the sun's descent, and called an end to the day's labor.

Gavin had spent the day flitting from one work site to another, his casted arm a glaring symbol of his impotence. He offered advice, ran small errands, and tried to make himself useful, but each rejection chipped away at his usual optimism. By evening, he was on his bunk, fast asleep.

The family washed up and gathered once more around the great oak table, their faces a mosaic of fatigue and fulfillment.

Supper was a quieter affair than the night before. The Becketts spoke in soft tones, conserving what little energy they had left. Plates were piled high with meatloaf and mashed potatoes, portions fit for a crew of loggers. Lilian had delivered the same fare to the bunkhouse, the older hands and boys digging in before she closed the door behind her.

"Glad to get the winter preparations over," said Annalee, yawning.

"We got a lot done," Grayson acknowledged. "But always more to do."

"Always is," said Jolene, patting his hand. "But we can breathe a bit now."

Joshua surveyed the tired but content faces of his family. This was what he loved most about ranch life. The tangible results of hard work always drew them all closer together.

Parker's mention of the mountain lion cut through the comfortable haze like a knife. "Heard a mountain lion today," he said, spearing a piece of meatloaf with his fork. "Cried like a baby."

Grayson nodded. "Probably the same one who caused Gavin's horse to buck. Big male, from the looks of him."

Speculation buzzed around the table. Annalee wondered if the lion was desperate enough to come down into the valley for livestock, while Lilian asked whether the men should take turns standing watch at night.

"It's nature," said Nathan, his tone more philosophical than usual. "The lion's trying to survive. We can't fault him for that."

"No, but we can be prepared," Naomi said, her voice cutting through Nathan's musing. "Losing a calf is one thing. Losing a horse or one of us is another."

Jolene looked at Joshua. "Is that the same lion that spooked Gavin's horse?"

"Might be," he answered. "We didn't get a good look at it."

The table fell silent, each person lost in their own calculations and concerns.

"Do you really think it's the same one?" Lilian asked, breaking the silence.

"Could be," said Grayson. "Or it could be a different cat altogether. Either way, we need to be vigilant."

Naomi leaned back in her chair, crossing her arms. "We've dealt with lions before. This isn't anything new."

Joshua listened, absorbing the varying degrees of concern and bravado. His thoughts drifted to Faith again, wondering what she was doing tonight, alone in her large house. The idea bothered him.

The family finished their meal in contemplative silence, each member slowly piecing together the days ahead.

Joshua couldn't shake the feeling the lion was more than an animal threat. He believed it was a harbinger of something larger. A test for them all.

Chapter Five

Faith Goodell opened her front door wide, letting the crisp autumn air rush in along with a flurry of eager women. She greeted each with a gracious smile, directing them toward the parlor, where a table of refreshments and chairs had been arranged. The women shrugged off coats and hats, chatting excitedly amongst themselves.

This was the first official meeting of the Mystic Women's Alliance, and the air was thick with anticipation.

"Thank you all for coming," Faith called out. "Make yourselves comfortable."

The women took their seats, some perched on the edges of their chairs, as if ready to spring into action. Faith surveyed the room, her heart swelling. These were the women who would help shape the future of Mystic—business owners, mothers, and teachers—all united by a common goal. The room buzzed with the sound of passionate voices and clinking teacups.

A knock at the door momentarily hushed the

crowd. Faith opened it to find Naomi and Annalee Beckett standing on her stoop. She blinked in surprise.

"Naomi, Annalee. I didn't expect to see you here. Please, come inside."

Annalee flashed her trademark confident grin. "You know we support what you're doing, Faith."

Naomi nodded, her expression more reserved but no less committed. "It's important work. We want to help."

Faith's surprise melted into genuine pleasure. "I'm so glad. Your presence means a lot."

The Becketts were an institution in Mystic. Their support could sway others who were on the fence, giving the alliance the legitimacy it sorely needed. Faith ushered them inside, where the other women greeted them with a mix of respect and curiosity.

With the Becketts here, the Alliance suddenly felt more formidable, more real.

For a brief interlude, the women turned their attention to the refreshments laid out on a side table. Maisy and Aggie had outdone themselves, providing an array of sweet breads, fruit bars, coffee, and a large pot of steaming tea. The women mixed and mingled, forming small knots of conversation as they filled their plates and cups.

"It's wonderful to see so many women interested in the Alliance," said Melody Jennings, her voice carrying over the hum of the room.

Faith circulated, making sure everyone was introduced and felt welcome. She paused to speak with

Annalee, then moved on to exchange a few words with Mia Duval, the newcomer from New Orleans who had recently joined their ranks.

The pleasant atmosphere did more than fill stomachs. The informal conversations built bridges. The women settled into their chairs, eyes bright with expectation.

As Faith prepared to start the formal proceedings, the front door opened once more. A tall man with dark hair and a rugged manner stepped in, removing his hat.

"Ladies," Doyle Shaw said with a nod.

An uneasy silence settled over the room. Some of the women exchanged glances, their expressions a mixture of suspicion and curiosity. Others, like Melody Jennings, offered more welcoming smiles.

"We're glad you could make it, Doyle," Faith said, though she sounded a bit uncertain. Shaw was the owner of the Starlight Saloon and had a reputation for being progressive. Then again, he was still a man, and this was meant to be a women's gathering.

"I won't stay long," Shaw said. "Just wanted to show my support and see how I might assist."

The women murmured among themselves. Having Doyle on their side could be invaluable, but there was also the fear he might twist their words or intentions.

For now, they tolerated his presence, knowing he could be an ally or a hindrance.

Faith stood, and the room fell silent. Doyle Shaw leaned against a wall, folding his arms and watching with interest.

"Ladies, we have a lot to discuss," Faith began, her voice measured. "This is just the start, but it's an important one. Our goal is to give the women of Mystic a voice in our businesses and in our community."

She pointed to a large piece of blank newsprint tacked to the wall, covered in neat handwriting. It listed various topics. Taxes, business growth, voting rights, the children's fund, and opening a library were issues most women were interested in addressing.

"These are some of the issues we might tackle. Your input is crucial."

The women leaned in, their faces set with interest as they read the topics.

Aggie Price was the first to speak. "The new taxes the all-male council voted in are hurting small businesses. I don't mind paying a fair share for town improvements, but if we don't get some relief soon, many of us won't last another year."

Melody Jennings countered. "While taxes are a concern, we need to think long-term. The right to vote affects everything else."

"Can we do both?" asked Annalee, her eagerness cutting through the more seasoned women's pragmatism. "Tackle immediate issues while working toward the bigger picture?"

Different voices chimed in, each woman bringing her own perspective and experience to the table. Evelyn Graham, the town's teacher, spoke passionately about the children's fund, while Mia Duval made a case for legal protections for women.

Doyle Shaw listened to the ideas and comments, his presence a constant reminder their words could reach beyond this room.

Their enthusiasm was contagious, spreading through the room like wildfire.

After nearly an hour of vigorous debate, Faith held up her hands for silence. "It's clear we have many important issues to address. For now, let's vote on the priority of each one."

She passed around small slips of paper and a tin for collecting them. The women scribbled quickly, some whispering to their neighbors, others casting furtive glances at the Becketts or Shaw.

Faith tallied the votes aloud. "Taxes... four. Children's fund... three. Library... five. Voting rights... six."

A murmur ran through the crowd. While some had hoped for a different outcome, it was clear most agreed on the fundamental importance of suffrage.

"So, we start with the right to vote," Faith said. "Are we all in agreement?"

"Hold on," Melody Jennings said, standing. "We need to be smart about this."

All eyes turned to Melody, who dabbed at the corner of her mouth with a lace handkerchief. "I'm not saying we back down on the important issue of getting the right to vote. However, perhaps we start with something less contentious. Build some goodwill and momentum first."

"Such as?" Annalee asked, a hint of skepticism in

her voice.

"Opening a library," Melody said. "It's something everyone can get behind. Imagine the knowledge and resources it would provide. Once we've established ourselves with a popular project, we'll be in a stronger position to tackle the tougher issues."

Gloria Graham, seated next to Melody, nodded in agreement. "It's a pragmatic approach. We need the community's support, and this could be a way to earn it. Rushing headlong into the most controversial issues could splinter our Alliance before it even gets started."

The room grew quiet as the women considered their words.

Some of the women shifted uncomfortably in their seats, not wanting to seem as if they were backing down from the fight. But Gloria's words carried weight. As the wife of the bank president and member of the town council, she understood the intricacies of community politics.

"If we can show them we are reasonable and thoughtful in our approach," Gloria continued, "we'll be more likely to gain the support we need."

The women began to murmur, their initial hesitation giving way to a growing sense of agreement.

"Imagine having access to a wide range of books," said Evelyn Graham, daughter of the bank president. "I believe what Melody and Gloria are saying makes sense."

Annalee spoke up next. "A library would benefit everyone. It's something we can point to as a tangible accomplishment."

The enthusiasm for the library grew, with women suggesting book drives and fundraising ideas. Even Doyle Shaw looked impressed.

Naomi Beckett raised her hand, and the room fell silent. "If we're serious about this, I can offer space in one of the buildings we own. It's not being used for anything at the moment, and it would save us the trouble of finding a location."

The women turned to Naomi, their eyes widening with hope and gratitude.

"That's very generous, Naomi," Faith said, beaming. "Having a space will make all the difference."

Doyle Shaw cleared his throat, catching Faith's eye. "If it's worth anything, I'll start the fund with fifty dollars."

A collective gasp went up, followed by applause. Even the more skeptical women couldn't hide their appreciation for Shaw's gesture. Having a successful business owner behind the idea, plus his significant donation, gave the library project an immediate boost.

"Thank you, Doyle," Faith said, genuinely touched. "Your support means a great deal."

Shaw nodded, accepting the thanks with modesty. "Just doing my part, ladies."

Perhaps Doyle Shaw wasn't such a bad egg after all, Faith thought.

With the major discussions concluded, Faith looked at the clock on her mantle. "We still have a bit of time. Let's elect our officers."

The women looked at each other, some leaning back as if to distance themselves from the process, others sitting up straighter, ready to volunteer. Faith passed around more slips of paper and the tin, and the women quickly cast their votes.

"First, for president," Faith said. "Mr. Shaw, perhaps you would count the votes and announce the name for each position."

"I'd be honored." Walking to stand next to Faith, he opened the tin and read the slips, noting each position and the names on a piece of paper. "Faith Goodell is your first president of the Alliance."

She blushed as the women applauded. "Well, thank you. I accept."

The results for the other positions came swiftly. Doyle cleared his throat before continuing. "Vice president is Melody Jennings. Secretary is Maisy Cox. Treasurer is Mia Duval. And at-large committee members are Gloria Graham and Naomi Beckett."

Each woman accepted her role, and a few of the women rose to give them hugs and congratulations.

They had a plan, they had leadership, and most importantly, they had a group of women committed to being involved.

The meeting adjourned, and the women gathered their belongings, still talking excitedly about the library and their new Alliance. Faith walked to the door and opened it, letting the cool air rush in.

What she saw outside made her stop short. A group of men—ten or twelve—stood on the walkway, their postures rigid and confrontational. Among them, Faith recognized several prominent townsfolk: Farley Byrne, owner of Mystic Feed and Grain, Elmer Moss, the town barber, Attorney Braxton Reed, and Casper Jennings, Melody's husband. Casper's presence was a huge surprise.

The women filed out, their conversations tapering off as they realized what awaited them. One by one, they paused and took stock of the situation, their earlier optimism colliding with the stark reality of the opposition they now faced.

The men's faces were flushed with irritation, their bodies tense with purpose.

The women held back, unsure whether to confront the men or simply wait them out. Whispers of "What do they want?" and "This can't be good," floated through the group.

Evelyn Graham muttered to no one in particular. "I thought Casper would be supportive, given Melody's involvement."

Maisy shrugged, her usual cheerfulness dampened. "Maybe he's here to protect her. Or maybe she didn't tell him."

Mia Duval, ever the analytical mind, observed, "It's one thing to have their wives express an opinion. It's another for us to organize."

Faith lingered at the doorway, her thoughts racing. Were they truly prepared for this kind of resistance? The Alliance had seemed like such a noble, straightforward endeavor just an hour ago. Now, the path ahead looked much more perilous.

Faith squared her shoulders and stepped forward,

her heart pounding in her chest. Raising a hand, she signaled for the women to wait. "Is there something you'd like to say?" she called out to the men.

Farley Byrne stepped forward. "We hear you're planning to stir up trouble," he said, his voice clipped.

"We're just trying to improve our community," Faith replied, struggling to keep her tone even.

"Your community?" Farley scoffed. "What about your families? Your husbands? They're what's important."

The tension was palpable, like the charged air before a lightning strike. The women behind Faith stood in silent solidarity, waiting to see how this first test would play out.

"We want what's best for everyone," Faith said, her voice firm.

Then Doyle Shaw made his way through the women to stand next to Faith. "Gentlemen, let me assure you the women do have the best interests of the community in mind. Their first project is to establish a library in town. To start off, Naomi Beckett has donated a space in town, and I'm putting up fifty dollars as seed money. What are you men willing to offer in support of such an important endeavor?"

The men grumbled, their dissatisfaction far from resolved. One by one, they began to disperse, but the threat lingered in the cold night air. As they left the area, one man continued to stand toward the back of the group.

Arms crossed over his chest, his booted feet shoulder width apart, Joshua Beckett locked eyes with Faith.

Chapter Six

Faith descended the porch steps with the grace of someone on a mission. Joshua waited at the gate, his posture relaxed yet wary. Without a word, she linked her arm through his, and they set off down the main street.

The town of Mystic showed little activity on this Sunday afternoon. A shopkeeper swept the board-walk with no intention of opening his store on a clear, crisp day. A mother herded children toward the family's wagon.

Joshua and Faith made an imposing pair, the slender woman and the tall rancher, striding with purpose.

"Thank you for coming," she said, breaking the silence.

"I wasn't planning on it until I saw the group of men standing outside your house," Joshua replied.

They walked at a relaxed pace. Faith glanced up at Joshua, searching his face. He met her gaze, and for a moment, it seemed he might say something more.

Instead, he simply nodded, and she understood. Whatever his thoughts, he was here for her.

"Miss Goodell," called a stout man from the doorway of the hardware store. "You reckon a library will put food on folks' tables?"

Faith slowed, but Joshua urged her onward with a gentle tug. "Guess we'll find out when the library opens, Mr. Harkins," she called back, not missing a step.

"Balance," Joshua murmured. "That's the tricky part."

She shot him a sidelong glance. "You think it's impossible?"

"I think it's hard," he said. "Hard isn't the same as impossible."

They passed the closed clinic, where a cluster of men eyed Faith with a mix of curiosity and disapproval. One of them hollered after them. "How's the voting issue going, Faith? Ever think about what your pa would say about what you're stirring up?"

Faith's grip on Joshua's arm tightened. He could feel the tension radiating from her, the conflict between her fiery spirit and the calculated restraint she knew was needed.

"We're making progress," she stated, more to herself than to the man who now stood behind them.

Joshua remained silent, his thoughts unreadable. Faith wondered if he agreed with the skeptics or if he believed in her cause but not in her ability to see it through. Yet he walked with her, and that meant something.

Each doubt cast her way was meant to be a gust of wind trying to snuff out a candle. Instead, it made Faith's flame dance higher.

They turned a corner, where the trees lining the road had begun to shed their autumn colors. Leaves swirled around their feet like a playful dog's tail.

"The meeting went better than I expected," Faith said. "I'm proud of how the women came together. A library is something tangible, a benefit to everyone."

Joshua nodded. "It's a sensible compromise. How do you plan to run it?"

"Donations at first. Books, money, whatever people can spare. We hope the Alliance members will volunteer their time to keep it open several days a week."

"Hope?" Joshua raised an eyebrow.

"Expect," she corrected herself, then sighed. "It's a lot to ask. These women have families and businesses. It will be difficult for them to carve out more time to volunteer in the library."

"They wouldn't be part of the Alliance if they didn't believe in what you're doing."

Faith considered this. "Belief is one thing. Sacrifice is another."

They walked in silence for a moment, the sound of fall leaves crunching underfoot filling the space between them. Faith unlinked her arm from Joshua's and crossed her arms over her chest as if hugging herself against an unseen chill.

"We're setting the foundation for something lasting," she said, her voice full of conviction. "I just hope the future cares to build on it."

They neared the edge of town, where buildings gave way to open fields.

"Doyle Shaw," he said, breaking the quiet. "Why was he at the meeting?"

She unclasped her arms and let them swing freely at her sides. "He wanted to hear our ideas firsthand. He's been supportive."

"Supportive," Joshua repeated, his tone neutral.

"He dispersed the group of men who were loitering outside, remember? Those men weren't there to cheer us on. Doyle's a businessman. He knows which way the wind is blowing."

"So, you think his support isn't genuine?"

"I think it's pragmatic."

They reached a small park where a few children played on makeshift swings. An older boy ran barefoot, a kite trailing behind him like a conquered dragon. Faith slowed, then stopped, causing Joshua to turn and face her.

"We need all the allies we can get," she said.

He held her gaze for a long moment. "Be careful who you trust."

He started walking again. Faith hesitated, then hurried to catch up, her mind whirring with the implications of Joshua's words. Allies, trust, pragmatism. She weighed each concept like a reporter sifting through facts for a story.

Joshua slowed his pace, and Faith matched him, their strides becoming more deliberate.

"You know," he began, "attending the open council meetings would be a good start. Listening, learning. It might make the men more comfortable with the idea of you having a say.”

“We don’t just want to listen, Joshua. We want to participate.”

“And you will, in time. Look at Grayson. He didn’t just walk in and take a seat. He attended meetings from the time he returned to the ranch, got to know the issues, the people. Now, he’s in a position where he can influence things, such as the proposed tax for the schoolhouse addition.”

Faith’s interest piqued. “A schoolhouse tax?”

“The council is split. Some think the business tax is necessary. Others believe it’ll be too much of a burden. Grayson suggested gathering donations and volunteers to build the addition instead. It’s more work, but it won’t strain anyone’s purse.”

“Sounds reasonable.”

“It is. And the kind of approach that wins people over. Reasonable, gradual. If the women start showing up, expressing your concerns, you’ll begin to sway opinions.”

Faith considered his words. “So, you think we should put our efforts into attending meetings instead of pushing for the vote directly?”

“Starting with the meetings shows you’re serious and you understand the process. It’ll make your eventual issue of voting mean more.”

They walked in silence for a few moments, each lost in thought. A wagon trundled past, its driver tipping his hat to the pair.

"One step at a time, Faith," Joshua said. "Be patient. You'll get there."

They circled back toward her house, the crisp air tinged with the scent of wood smoke from early afternoon hearths.

"Grayson's approach makes sense," Faith said. "People are more willing to give when they see where their contributions are going. It creates a sense of ownership, of community."

"Exactly. The council isn't against the addition. They need to find a way to do it without hurting the people they're trying to help. Sometimes, the simplest solution isn't the best one."

Faith pondered this. "So, you think the women should oppose the tax?"

"I think you should support solutions that achieve the same goal without creating more problems. If you stand with Grayson on this, it shows you're thinking beyond your own immediate needs."

"Alliances," Faith said, more to herself than to Joshua. She was beginning to see the larger picture, the intricate web of relationships and interests governing the town.

"Attend the next open meeting. Bring as many women as you can and state your preference. Your presence alone will speak volumes."

Faith stopped walking and turned to Joshua. His tall frame might intimidate some women. She didn't flinch. Instead, she studied him, wondering if he saw her as more than his outspoken friend, if he recognized the depth of her ambition and the challenges she faced.

Faith offered a confident smile. "We'll be there."

They walked in companionable silence back toward her house.

"I'm glad we talked," she said.

"So am I," Joshua replied. "You know I want what's best for the town. And for you."

"For me?" Faith teased, raising an eyebrow.

"Absolutely." A small smile played on his lips. "For all the women in Mystic. The families. Everyone."

They reached her house, where Joshua had tied his horse, Jupiter. The dapple-gray gelding nickered softly at the sight of Joshua.

"We've always been friends, haven't we?" Faith asked, taking a step back from Joshua.

"Since we started school," he answered.

"Our friendship won't change, will it? Even if we don't always see eye to eye?"

He paused, then turned to face her. "Friendship isn't about agreeing on everything, Faith. It's about understanding. And standing by each other."

Relief washed over her. "I'm glad to hear that."

Joshua mounted Jupiter, the horse shifting its weight in anticipation. "Take care, Faith," he said, tipping his hat.

"As you, Joshua."

As Jupiter's hooves took them toward the ranch, Faith watched them grow smaller, fainter, like the receding echoes of a heartbeat.

Faith stood for a moment longer, watching, until

he was a speck in the distance. Their conversation replayed in her mind, each word and pause taking on new significance. Joshua had doubts, yes, but he'd also given her valuable insights and, most important-ly, his support.

Turning toward her house, she walked up the steps to her front door. The house loomed like a sentinel over her dreams, its weathered facade a testament to the struggles and triumphs of her parents. Her father had fought similar battles, she reminded herself, and had often faced resistance from those who feared change.

Inside, the familiar sights welcomed her like an old friend. She walked to the desk in the parlor. Thoughts of the library, the tax, the upcoming council meeting swirled in her head.

Never one to sit idly and wait for the future to unfold, Faith pulled a sheet of stationery from a drawer and picked up a pen, tapping it thoughtfully against her chin. She began to write, the pen scratch-ing out elegant curves and lines.

Dear Alliance Board Members,

We need to convene before the next council meeting. There are important matters to dis-cuss, including the library and the proposed schoolhouse tax. I've received some insightful advice I believe could help us make a stronger case.

Let's meet at my house on Tuesday even-ing. Your presence and input are crucial.

Sincerely,
Faith

She read over the letter twice, making sure her words conveyed the urgency without causing alarm. The Alliance was dedicated, but it was also fragile.

She hoped they would see the wisdom in Joshua's suggestion and not view it as a retreat.

There was one more place Joshua needed to stop by before riding back to the ranch. He reined in Jupiter outside the Starlight Saloon. The building was one of the oldest in Mystic, its wooden planks bleached and cracked from years of Montana sun. He swung a leg over the saddle, then paused, considering what he wanted to say before entering.

Pushing through the saloon doors, he was greeted by the mixed aromas of tobacco, whiskey, and sweat. As expected for a Sunday afternoon, the room was sparsely populated.

Doyle Shaw stood at the bar, his broad-shouldered frame hunched over a glass of amber liquid. He didn't appear to be drinking heavily, content to take sips with the leisure of a man who had time to kill. His eyes tracked a group of men playing cards in the corner, but his mind seemed elsewhere.

"Doyle," Joshua said, approaching the bar. The saloon owner turned, a smile breaking through his dark features.

"Joshua Beckett. What brings you here?"

Joshua tilted his head toward the card players. "Checking on Nathan."

Doyle followed Joshua's gaze. "Your brother's holding his own."

"Never doubted he would."

An awkward silence settled between them. Joshua broke it first. "Need to talk to you. About Faith."

Doyle gestured toward an empty table, but Joshua remained standing.

"What about Faith?" Doyle asked, leaning back slightly, his posture less inviting.

"She's grateful for your support," Joshua said. "We all are."

"That sounds like there's a 'but' coming."

Joshua studied Doyle for a moment, weighing his words. "She needs to know your support is real and not just for show."

Doyle's eyes narrowed. "You think I'm playing some kind of game?"

"I think you're smart enough to understand the risks. The women are putting a lot on the line, and they need to know they can count on the people who say they're with them."

Doyle swirled his drink. "I grew up with strong women, Joshua. My mother, my sisters. I respect what Faith is trying to do."

"Respect is good," Joshua said. "Trust is better."

The two men locked eyes, each measuring the other. Joshua broke first, turning to leave. "Just remember," he said over his shoulder, "if you betray their trust, you're not just crossing them. You're crossing all of us."

Chapter Seven

Joshua pushed through the saloon doors, and the afternoon light momentarily blinded him. He took a deep breath of the cool, crisp air, a stark contrast to the smoky warmth inside. Walking to Jupiter, he grabbed the reins and patted the horse's neck.

Inside, Doyle returned his gaze to the card players, his mind was elsewhere. He drained the last of his drink and signaled the bartender for a refill. The normally boisterous saloon owner was uncharacteristically quiet, his thoughts running deep.

Joshua lingered by the hitching post, listening to the muted sounds of the town. He had no illusions about Doyle. The man was as canny as they came, and his motivations were often layered. Mystic was a small town, and alliances, whether political, social, or personal, had a way of intertwining.

Doyle lifted his refreshed glass and stared into it as if seeking answers in the swirling liquid. The card players laughed and shouted, oblivious to the storm brewing in one man's conscience.

Outside, Joshua swung into the saddle, casting one last glance at the saloon. He couldn't see Doyle from his vantage, but he imagined the man still standing at the bar, still pondering what was said.

Joshua reined Jupiter toward the ranch, trotting down the street to leave the quiet town behind. Doyle had supported the Alliance so far. Joshua knew trust was a fragile thing, easily shattered and hard to repair. As the peacemaker in the Beckett family, he felt as if he'd spent a lifetime mending broken bonds.

The ride back to the ranch would give him time to think about Faith, about the Alliance, about how all these changing dynamics in town would affect his family. For now, though, he let the rhythm of Jupiter's gait and the familiar sights of the countryside soothe his mind.

In the saloon, Doyle set his drink down, untouched. He rose slowly, with the heavy deliberation of a man carrying a newfound burden, and walked to the large front windows. He watched as Joshua Beckett rode away, the rancher's silhouette growing smaller against the backdrop of the waking town.

Doyle had decisions to make. The kind that could change the course of friendships, of alliances, of lives.

Faith Goodell stood on her porch, the chill of evening whispered across her skin. Her gaze was locked on Joshua Beckett, who approached through her gate, his figure outlined by the rising moon.

"Evening, Faith," he said, tipping his hat in a gesture of familiarity and respect.

"Evening, Joshua." She turned to open the front door, stepping inside ahead of him.

"Thank you for coming. I thought it best if you could explain your thoughts on the Alliance moving forward."

"I'm glad you invited me," he replied.

Faith ushered him into the parlor. The room was already filled with the low murmur of conversation. The discussions stopped, replaced by greetings when Joshua appeared. He smiled, letting it linger on his mother, who sat next to Gloria Graham, a woman Naomi professed to take with a grain of salt.

They took their seats, and Faith felt a surge of pride looking around the room. The women who gathered on a Tuesday evening were the embodiment of resilience and strength.

Melody Jennings leaned forward. "So, what is the purpose of this meeting, Faith?" The others nodded, anxious to hear the topic.

She took a deep breath, her eyes scanning the room. "We've already decided to organize a library in the building Naomi Beckett graciously offered." She nodded at Naomi. "We have fifty dollars from Doyle Shaw to get started. This is a topic I've asked Mayor Jurgen to place on the council's agenda for Friday. He agreed. However, there are matters we should discuss prior to their meeting."

A few eyebrows rose, but most faces showed a

spark of excitement. Faith pushed forward, her voice gaining momentum.

"We'll need volunteers to keep it open several days a week. I would suggest we settle this in case the town council asks."

"I can help on most Saturday mornings," Naomi offered in her no-nonsense voice.

"And I can do one morning a week," Melody said.

The women continued to volunteer until they had coverage for Wednesday, Thursday, Friday, and Saturday mornings.

Faith smiled. "Thank you. All of you. I'm certain some of the other members will be able to volunteer, also."

Joshua listened, admiring the dedication of each woman. Yet a part of his mind wandered to the broader implications of their efforts.

Faith looked around the room before changing the subject. "Joshua, please tell us your thoughts on the proposed tax for the schoolhouse addition."

He leaned forward. "The council wants to levy a tax to fund the schoolhouse addition. This tax would be levied on businesses until enough money is collected to pay for the work. My brother and town council member, Grayson, has another idea. He thinks we should gather donations and seek able-bodied volunteers to build the addition without imposing a tax."

Maisy Cox's eyes brightened. "That's a wonderful idea. It doesn't burden the business owners and brings the community together."

Joshua smiled. "Exactly. But it needs support from the townsfolk."

"We'll support it," Gloria Graham said with conviction. "The Alliance can gather donations and even volunteer some labor if needed."

A round of agreement circled the group.

Joshua continued. "It would help if you attended the next open council meeting. Bring as many women as you can. Show you're invested in this issue, too."

Again, the women agreed and offered to talk with other Alliance members to encourage them to attend the council meeting.

Faith's gaze met his, and for a moment, they shared an unspoken understanding. "We'll be there," she promised.

The meeting continued with discussions on logistics, fundraising, and volunteer schedules. As the plans solidified, Faith felt the weight of skepticism lift, replaced by a growing sense of purpose.

After the meeting adjourned, Faith and Joshua stepped back outside.

"Thank you for being here," Faith said, her voice soft with gratitude.

"Anytime, Faith," Joshua replied.

They walked back to the path where Naomi waited atop her horse.

As they reached the spot where Jupiter stood, Faith turned to Joshua. "I'm glad we talked. And I'm glad we're friends."

He smiled, a genuine warmth in his eyes. "Me, too, Faith. And remember, no matter what, we'll always be friends."

Faith nodded, feeling a swell of emotion. "I'll see you soon. Be safe."

"You, too," he replied, mounting his gelding with practiced ease.

Faith waved to Naomi, watching as they rode away. She stood there a moment before turning and heading back toward her house. Instead of thinking about the meeting, her mind stayed on Joshua. He'd been in her thoughts more and more, even keeping her awake some nights.

A bright, incredibly attractive man, she'd wondered for a while why he'd never shown much interest in courting any of the single women in town. At one time, she was certain he planned to court a young woman who'd come to town with her parents. It didn't happen.

Faith wondered how she would respond if he showed her more interest beyond their lifelong friendship. The thought sent spikes of fear into her heart. But... what if...?

Forcing herself to stop thinking about Joshua, as if she were a schoolgirl, she thought back to tonight's meeting. Joshua's words rang with clarity, and she knew the Mystic Women's Alliance needed to show a united front at the next council meeting.

Sun filtered through the lace curtains, creating

delicate patterns across Faith's room. She stretched, feeling the pleasant pull of relaxed muscles, and sat up.

She dressed quickly, the fabric of her wool dress warming her chilled skin. In the small kitchen, she prepared a breakfast of coffee, eggs, and toasted biscuits. The comforting aroma of the coffee mingled with the crisp scent of morning air.

As she sat down to eat, her mind considered her plans for the day. Her fork clinked against her plate, the simple meal fueling both her body and mind for the day ahead.

Finishing, Faith washed the dishes and set them aside to dry. Slipping into her coat and wool hat, she stepped outside. The morning air was cool, though the sun carried the promise of warmth. The town of Mystic was already stirring, the sounds of daily life beginning to build into a familiar rhythm.

"On three," Joshua said in a commanding voice. Parker and Little Joe braced themselves, hands gripping the rough wood of a new barn door. "One, two, three!"

With a grunt of effort, they lifted the door from the ground, muscles straining under the weight. The cold air bit at their exposed skin, but they ignored it, focused on the task at hand. Slowly, carefully, they maneuvered the door into place, setting it against the frame with a satisfying thud.

"Thought we were gonna lose it there for a second," Parker said, breathing hard.

Joshua wiped sweat from his brow with the back of his hand. At six feet tall, he was the same height as Parker, but where his younger brother was lean and wiry, Joshua had the solid build of a man who'd spent his life working a ranch. The almost ten years between them made a difference in many ways.

"Don't celebrate yet," Joshua said. "We still need to get the hinges on."

Little Joe, a gangly fifteen-year-old with a shock of red hair, fidgeted with a set of tools. "I can handle the hinges, if you want," he offered.

Parker snorted. "The same as you handled the fence post last week?"

"That wasn't my fault," Little Joe protested. "The ground was frozen solid."

Joshua held up a hand to forestall the argument. "Let him have a go at it, Parker. We can always redo it if needed."

The camaraderie among the three was palpable. Even Little Joe, who wasn't a Beckett by blood, had been taken in as one of their own. They fell into an easy rhythm, each knowing their role, their light-hearted banter filling the air as they worked. Little Joe concentrated his efforts on the hinges, finally stepping back to examine them. A broad grin appeared.

Joshua inspected the door, giving it a few test swings. "Not bad," he said. "It's starting to come together. Good work, Joe."

They worked with renewed vigor, the prospect of a warm fire and hot meal spurring them on. The physical labor was intense, every muscle in their bodies protesting as they hurried to complete the task. Parker and Little Joe fell back into their usual pattern of teasing, their jabs at each other growing more creative and absurd with each passing minute.

As they laughed, Joshua's thoughts drifted like snowflakes, landing softly on the image of Faith Goodell.

Joshua's hands moved on autopilot as he considered the woman who'd occupied so many of his thoughts lately. Faith was nothing if not passionate, whether it was about the newspaper, her friends, or the town of Mystic itself. He admired her, even when he didn't always agree with her.

"Josh," Parker said, bringing him back to the present. "You gonna hold that or what?"

Joshua looked down to see he was holding a nail, completely forgetting to drive it in. "Sorry," he muttered, taking the hammer from Parker and giving the nail a few solid whacks.

"You're miles away," Parker said, eyeing his older brother. "Something on your mind?"

"Thinking about the ranch," Joshua lied. "About the future."

His thoughts immediately returned to Faith. How she laughed, how she challenged him, how she looked at him with such intensity he felt both exposed and understood.

He remembered the night of Cody's wedding, the two of them sitting on the porch of the homestead, watching the celebration wind down. She'd rested her head on his shoulder, and for a brief, terrifying moment, he'd wanted to kiss her. Instead, he'd made some awkward joke and stood up, leaving her confused and alone.

Years later, long after Cody's wife and daughter had been murdered, Joshua considered if he could even pursue something with Faith. The idea gnawed at him. A relationship with her wouldn't be simple or easy.

"You coming to the house, Josh?" Parker asked.

"You boys go on. I'll be there soon," he answered.

Joshua let the brisk air clear his mind. He took a seat on a bale of hay and rubbed his hands together, lost in thought. What did he really fear? Rejection, certainly. The sting of putting himself out there only to be turned down was something he wasn't sure he could handle.

The deeper dread, though, was the fear of losing what he and Faith had. Their friendship was important to him, a rock, no matter what troubles they faced.

How did she even feel about him? He could sometimes convince himself the looks she gave him, the touches, the way she spoke his name—all were signs of something more. Just as often, he doubted his interpretations, and worried he was seeing what he wanted to see rather than what was real.

He remembered Annalee's words from a few

weeks ago. "She's not going to wait around forever, you know." His sister had always been more perceptive than he gave her credit for, and her warning had struck a chord. If Faith did have feelings for him, how long would she harbor them in silence, hoping he'd make a move?

He wasn't blind to the attention she received from other men. Attorney Braxton Reed, the young banker from Bozeman, and a ranch hand from Tripp Lassiter's ranch. They were all vying for her in one way or another. So far, she'd remained aloof, but Joshua knew it was only a matter of time before she let someone in.

The thought of her with someone else tightened his chest, and Joshua realized he couldn't keep her waiting forever.

Chapter Eight

Naomi Beckett stood at the kitchen sink, her hands immersed in warm, soapy water as she rinsed the last of the breakfast dishes. The scene beyond the window was a picturesque landscape straight out of a painting. The vibrant sun rose over the majestic mountains and tranquil valley spreading out before her.

With a satisfied smile, Naomi dried her hands on a kitchen towel and turned toward her family gathered in the dining room.

"I believe we ought to take advantage of this fine weather," she said. "Let's ride to Millard's Park for the day. The river should be high enough for some good fishing."

Jolene, cradling her newborn son, Cody, in her arms, looked up from the table where she and Grayson were making a list of supplies for the upcoming week. "Sounds perfect. We could all use a little break."

Joshua, seated next to Faith Goodell, who'd

stopped by earlier with Evelyn Graham to drop off the latest edition of the Mystic Gazette and a large plate of cookies, nodded in agreement. "A day out could do us some good, Ma."

"Faith, Evelyn, you're welcome to join us. There's plenty of room, and it's always more fun with a bigger group."

"The week's paper is out, so I don't have to rush back to town. It sounds lovely," Faith said.

Evelyn's face lit up. "No school on Saturday." She smiled. "I'd love to come. It's been ages since I've been to the park."

"Settled then," Naomi said. "We'll leave in an hour. I'll pack food."

"I'll help," Annalee called out, followed by Faith and Evelyn also offering their help.

The group dispersed, each tending to their own preparations. Joshua walked up to Faith.

"I'll saddle horses for you and Evelyn. She won't be able to take her buggy out there."

"Thank you, Josh. I'll let her know."

The caravan set off with high spirits. Two pack horses held the food and fishing gear. The landscape was a patchwork of fading greens and browns, awaiting the first snow of the season.

Jolene rode next to Grayson with little Cody wrapped against her chest in a cradleboard. Behind them, Joshua rode with Faith, and Evelyn with Cody, and the rest of the group behind them.

"Can you believe this weather? It's cold but so beautiful," Evelyn said.

Joshua glanced over at her. "Let's hope it holds."

The trail to Millard's Park wound through low hills and along the riverbank. The cottonwoods swayed in the light breeze. As they neared the park, a broad meadow bisected by the river, the sound of rushing water grew louder.

Cody Beckett nudged his horse forward, catching up with Grayson. "I'm not sure it's a good idea to stay long," he said, his voice carrying a note of concern. "The sky to the west looks like it's brewing something."

Grayson glanced toward the darkening horizon. "We'll keep an eye on it," he said.

They reined to a stop under a stand of trees, and the group set to unloading their gear. Fishing rods were set against tree trunks, blankets spread out, and baskets opened to reveal an array of food. The ranch hands dashed toward the river, only to be called back by Grayson.

"See if you can help out, then you'll need to dig up worms before you can fish."

The boys whooped in excitement before helping Naomi and Jolene unpack the food.

Evelyn approached Cody, who was checking the line on each fishing pole. "Do you think the fish will be biting today?" she asked.

He didn't look up. "Probably," he said, his tone

flat.

Undeterred, she continued. "I remember you teaching me how to cast right over there," she said, pointing to a bend in the river. "You were so patient."

Cody finished his knot and stood, rod in hand. "That was a long time ago," he said, then walked toward the river, leaving Evelyn standing alone.

Joshua observed the exchange from a distance. "You coming?" Faith said, interrupting his thoughts. She held two fishing rods, one extended toward him.

"Sure," he said, taking the rod and following her to the riverbank.

The morning passed in a leisurely fashion. The younger boys took turns swimming in the frigid water and fishing, the adults alternating between casting lines and lounging on the blankets. Cody caught the first fish, a sizable trout, and handed it off to one of the orphans without a word. Jolene and Grayson stole a few moments of quiet time, and Naomi kept a watchful eye on the whole scene, her expression softening.

An hour after noon, a low rumble echoed through the valley. The group looked up to see the once distant storm clouds now looming threateningly close, their edges flickering with lightning.

"Time to pack up!" Naomi called. "Move quickly!"

The serene picnic transformed into a flurry of activity. Blankets were shaken out and stuffed into bags. Fishing rods were stowed. The first fat raindrops began to fall as the group rushed to mount their horses.

"We're going to get soaked," Evelyn said, swinging up and into the saddle.

Faith wiped a wet strand of hair from her face. "We sure are."

They started for home, the trail already slick from the brief burst of rain. The storm hit in full force moments later, sheets of water driven by gusting winds. The sound of thunder drowned out attempts at conversation, and the group hunkered down, powerless against the onslaught.

The trail became a mire, the horses slowing in the deepening muck. Grayson shifted in the saddle to yell back to Joshua. "We need to take it slow. The horses are slipping."

Naomi, riding behind Jolene and Grayson, turned to see Gavin struggling to control the horse with one good arm. "Gavin, rein up!" She dropped back and took the reins. "You get on behind Samuel." A few minutes later, they were moving again, with Naomi ponying Gavin's horse.

The rain was a curtain, the trail ahead barely visible. A flash of lightning illuminated the landscape, followed by an immediate crack of thunder, spooking the horses.

Jolene shot a look at little Cody, who was tied to a cradleboard and secured to his father. The horses whinnied as they took a bend in the trail, sensing they were close to the homestead.

"We're almost there," Naomi yelled, her voice barely audible over the storm.

The group was drenched, their clothes clinging to

them like second skins. Faces were streaked with rain and mud, eyes fixed on the trail ahead. They were almost home.

The warmth of the Beckett homestead was a stark contrast to the cold, wet world outside. The group filed in, dripping and shivering, forming puddles on the wooden floor.

"Get the fire going," Naomi instructed Nathan and Parker. "Annalee, let's find some towels."

The house was a bustle of activity as wet clothes were peeled off and hung to dry. Annalee and Lilian distributed towels and offered spare garments to Faith and Evelyn.

"These should keep you warm until your clothes dry," Annalee said, handing Evelyn a simple cotton dress.

Evelyn accepted the dress with a grateful smile. "Thank you, Annalee. This is perfect."

"You're welcome. I need to find Faith and give her these." Annalee held up the clothes for Faith.

In the kitchen, Naomi and Jolene prepared a meal. The smell of hot biscuits and simmering stew filled the air, mingling with the scent of wet earth clinging to the almost dry clothes.

The large dining table in the Becketts' main room was set with mismatched China and napkins made of the extra fabric left from making a dress. It was an inviting sight. The family and their guests took seats, settling into the warm glow of the fire and the comfort of each other's company.

Faith, wearing one of Annalee's dresses, sat next to Joshua. He looked at her longer than usual, as if committing something to memory. She noticed, of course, and wondered what was going on in his head.

Evelyn found herself seated next to Cody. She hesitated for a moment before sitting down. "Cody," she said. "It's good to see you. I mean that."

He didn't answer right away, instead focusing on ladling stew into his bowl. "You're persistent."

"I just care, is all. A lot of people care about you."

He met her eyes, and for a moment, she saw the old Cody, the one who laughed and joked, the one who was full of life. Turned out, it was only a flicker. "I know," he said, then started to eat.

The meal progressed with a mix of boisterous and casual conversation. The young boys contributed with stories and questions, the Beckett family responding with the patience and warmth of true kin. Laughter punctuated the talk, and for a while, the storm outside was forgotten.

Joshua watched Faith, noting how she interacted with his family, how she fit in, even with her initial reservations. When she caught him staring, she raised an eyebrow.

"What?" she asked.

"Nothing," he said, looking away. "Just thinking."

"About what?"

He shrugged. "About how nice it is to have you

here."

Faith didn't know how to respond. She liked Joshua. More than liked him, if she was honest. She also valued her independence, her ability to come and go as she pleased. His quiet declaration left her feeling both flattered and unsettled.

At the other end of the table, Evelyn made another attempt to engage Cody. "Do you think you'll stay at the ranch? Or are you planning to go back to the Marshal Service?"

Cody finished his stew and set his spoon down carefully. "I haven't decided," he said. "There's a lot to think about."

Evelyn nodded, chewing on her bottom lip. "Well, whatever you choose, I hope you find some peace."

Without a word, Cody stood and took his bowl to the kitchen. He didn't return to the table.

The storm outside intensified, the wind howling through the eaves, and rain lashing against the windows. The house had the feel of a fortress, the thick log walls and roaring fire providing a sense of security and refuge.

Grayson stood and raised a glass. "I'm thankful we're all safe and together. Here's to family and friends."

The table echoed with the clink of glasses and mugs, a moment of unity and gratitude shared by all.

As the meal wound down, Joshua leaned close to Faith. "Why did you really come today?"

"Because you mentioned me coming out this weekend. And Evelyn wanted to deliver the cookies."

He nodded, his lips curling into a grin. "I'm glad."

The group lingered at the table, not ready to break the spell of warmth and camaraderie. Conversations drifted from one topic to another, the voices of the younger boys growing sleepy and subdued.

Evelyn looked toward the kitchen, where Cody stood alone, staring out a window. She wondered if he was watching the storm or seeing something else, something only he could perceive. She turned back to the table, her thoughts heavy with concern for the man who had once been the husband of her best friend.

At the far end of the table, Joshua continued to send occasional glances at Faith. She sensed him watching her and sighed.

"Joshua, if you have something to say, please say it."

"I've been thinking about how long we've been friends. There are times I still see us as young children running around, playing behind the church, or out here in the fields. Lately, there are times when it seems I don't know you at all."

Faith opened her mouth to speak, then closed it, unsure of what to say. She cared a great deal about Joshua and believed he cared the same for her. But life was never simple. She had her work, her own set of principles, and personal dreams. Could she fit his world into hers, or hers into his?

The storm created a sense of tension and confinement within the house, as if the walls were closing in, forcing each person to confront their thoughts and feelings. The events of the day played out in their minds.

Naomi cleared her throat, breaking the silence. "It's late. Faith and Evelyn, you're staying the night, of course. Boys, grab blankets from the closet and find a spot to bed down. No use trying to get to the bunkhouse in this weather."

The group slowly dispersed, rising from the table with stretches and yawns. Little Joe, Samuel, Gavin, Jason, and Ted trooped off to find spots to bed down while the adults lingered in the kitchen a little while longer.

Joshua took Faith's hand. "You and Evelyn can share a room upstairs."

She squeezed his hand before gently pulling hers away, starting up the stairs behind Evelyn. "I'll see you in the morning."

As the group prepared to bed down for the night, a sudden knock came at the door, shocking everyone into alertness. They froze, listening.

The knock came again, more urgent this time.

Chapter Nine

The ranch house creaked and groaned under the assault of the fierce Montana storm. Lightning illuminated the darkened parlor in brief, electric bursts as the Beckett family and their guests made their way toward the stairs, ready to retire for the night.

As if on cue, a sudden, thunderous pounding on the front door caused everyone in the room to freeze. Grayson's eyes narrowed, and he moved with the swift precision of a man accustomed to danger. He reached for his six-shooter, which hung on a peg near the door, and motioned for Joshua and Nathan to do the same.

Joshua's gaze met Grayson's, a silent understanding passing between them. He reached for his own weapon. Nathan, the youngest of the three, followed suit, his usual carefree demeanor replaced by a focused intensity.

"Who could be out in this weather?" Naomi Beckett whispered, her brow furrowed with worry.

Grayson's jaw clenched. "We're about to find out, Ma. Everyone, stay back."

As the three advanced toward the door, Grayson considered who could be on their porch in such an inhospitable storm. Who would brave such a storm to reach their isolated ranch? A traveler seeking shelter? Or someone with nefarious intentions?

Another round of pounding shook the door in its frame.

"Whoever you are, state your business," Grayson called out, his voice raised to be heard over the storm.

The response was muffled by the wind, but the desperation in the voice was clear. "Please! I need help!"

Grayson exchanged a glance with Joshua, who gave a slow nod. Nathan's grip tightened on his pistol, his eyes alert and ready.

"I'm opening the door," Grayson announced, his free hand reaching for the latch. "But I warn you, we're armed."

With a deep breath, Grayson opened the door, revealing the storm-lashed night beyond. The wind howled into the house, bringing with it a spray of icy rain. And there, silhouetted against the tempest, stood a lone figure.

The figure before them was a man, drenched to the bone, his great coat clinging to his frame like a second skin. A wide-brimmed hat was pulled low over his head, obscuring most of his features, but Grayson could see the glint of desperate eyes peering out from beneath its brim.

"Good Lord," Grayson muttered, his stern bearing shaken by the sight. He quickly regained his composure, motioning the stranger inside with a sweep of his arm. "Come in, man, before you catch your death out there."

The stranger stumbled across the threshold, water pooling at his feet as he stood dripping in the entryway. Joshua and Nathan flanked their older brother, weapons still at the ready.

"Who are you?" Grayson demanded, his voice firm but not unkind. "And what brings you to Wild Spirit Ranch on a night like this?"

The stranger's hands, trembling slightly from the cold, reached up to remove his hat before pulling the sleeves of the great coat, letting it fall to the floor. As he did so, a shock of thick auburn hair was revealed, plastered to his forehead by the rain. His stark, gray-blue eyes met Grayson's, a mix of wariness and relief evident in their depths.

"Name's Trent Galloway," he said, his words crisp, despite the slight drawl. "I was caught in the storm, saw your place. I'm much obliged for the shelter."

Grayson studied the man for a moment, noting his lean but muscular build and the way he carried himself. Galloway was alert, even in his exhausted state. A man, Grayson guessed, accustomed to danger.

"I'm Grayson Beckett. These are my brothers, Joshua and Nathan."

Joshua nodded, his gaze assessing. Nathan, ever the friendly one, managed a quick smile.

Grayson weighed the potential risks against the basic human decency of offering aid to a stranger in need. The storm continued to rage outside, emphasizing the dire circumstances that brought this man to their door.

"You're welcome to dry off and warm up," Grayson finally said, his tone still cautious. "I hope you understand if we keep a close eye on you, Mr. Galloway. These are uncertain times, and we've got family to protect."

Trent Galloway nodded, a ghost of a smile touching his lips. "I'd expect nothing less, Mr. Beckett. You're wise to be cautious. I assure you, I mean no harm to you or yours. I'm just grateful for a roof over my head tonight."

As Grayson watched Galloway carefully remove his sodden boots, he couldn't shake the feeling this unexpected visitor was about to bring a whirlwind of change to Wild Spirit Ranch. One rivaling the storm still howling beyond their walls.

As the men stood in uneasy silence, the sound of determined footsteps drew their attention. Naomi Beckett emerged from the shadows of the hallway, her petite frame belying the strength in her bearing. Her light eyes, sharp and discerning, swept over the scene before settling on their unexpected guest.

Naomi stepped forward, positioning herself in front of her sons, a subtle yet unmistakable gesture of protection. "I'm Naomi Beckett, matriarch of this household. And you are?"

Trent Galloway offered a respectful nod to Naomi.

"Ma'am, I'm Trent Galloway. I apologize for the late intrusion."

Her eyes narrowed. "What brings you to these parts, Mr. Galloway? Our ranch isn't exactly on the way to anywhere."

Galloway's gaze met Naomi's, a flicker of admiration crossing his face at her directness. "Truth be told, Mrs. Beckett, I'm a bounty hunter. I'm on the trail of some men who robbed a bank in Helena not two weeks past."

A collective intake of breath filled the room. Joshua stepped forward, his interest piqued. "The Helena robbery? We heard about it. Took quite a haul, didn't they?"

Galloway nodded. "They did. And left two good men dead in the process. I aim to bring them to justice."

Naomi's brow furrowed, her mind working through the implications of harboring a bounty hunter who could potentially draw the attention of dangerous criminals. "And you think these men might be headed to Mystic?"

"I have reason to believe they're hiding out in this area," Galloway replied, his Texas drawl becoming more pronounced. "Hoping to lay low until the heat dies down."

Grayson exchanged a worried glance with his mother. The thought of such dangerous men so close to their home sent a chill down his spine. "How can you be sure?" he asked.

"I've been tracking them for days. Found some

evidence pointing this way."

"Mr. Galloway," she said, her tone leaving no room for argument, "I think it's time you told us everything you know about these men and why you believe they're here. Our hospitality comes at the price of your honesty."

The bounty hunter's eyes widened slightly, not expecting such forthrightness from the diminutive woman before him. A tense silence fell over the room as everyone waited to see how he would respond.

Naomi's piercing gaze bore into Trent Galloway, her resolve as unyielding as the Montana mountains surrounding them. The bounty hunter shifted his weight, his hand instinctively brushing the grip of his holstered pistol.

"Ma'am," Galloway began, his voice low and measured, "I respect your concern for your family and town. But some details of my investigation are a tetch sensitive."

Grayson stepped forward, his broad shoulders tense. "Mr. Galloway, we appreciate your position, but we need to know what kind of danger might be headed our way."

Naomi's weathered hands clenched at her sides as she wrestled with her conflicting instincts. The storm howled outside, punctuating the tense silence within.

"Despite my reservations, I can't in good conscience turn you out in this weather, Mr. Galloway." She turned to her daughter. "Annalee, prepare a place for our guest to sleep on the kitchen floor."

Annalee nodded, her youthful energy a stark contrast to the tension in the room. "Right away, Mama."

As Annalee bustled off, Naomi fixed Galloway with a stern look. "But understand this. Your presence here puts us all at risk. I expect you to share what information you have come morning."

"You have my word, Mrs. Beckett. And I'm grateful for your hospitality."

While Naomi busied herself preparing a late meal for their unexpected guest, Grayson pulled his brothers aside. "We can't be too careful," he murmured. "Joshua, Nathan, Cody—we'll take turns keeping watch through the night."

Joshua's brow furrowed. "Good idea."

"Better safe than sorry," Cody said. The bitterness in his eyes spoke of tragedy and loss.

Nathan nodded in agreement. "I'll take first watch."

As the storm's fury began to wane in the small hours of the morning, the Beckett brothers maintained their vigilant rotation. Each man's thoughts turned to the potential dangers lurking beyond their walls, and the mysterious stranger now sleeping under their roof.

The morning sun streamed through the windows of Wild Spirit Ranch, illuminating the bustling kitchen. Faith Goodell smoothed her skirt as she stepped into the room, her curious gaze drawn to the unfamiliar figure seated at the table.

"Faith, Evelyn. I don't believe you've met our visitor," Naomi Beckett called, gesturing toward the rugged man. "This is Mr. Trent Galloway. Trent, this is Evelyn Graham and Faith Goodell. They're good friends of our family."

Trent stood with a courteous nod. "Ladies, it's a pleasure."

Faith felt a flutter in her chest as she met Trent's piercing gaze. "Mr. Galloway." She ignored the unexpected warmth spreading through her.

As everyone settled around the table, the aroma of coffee and sizzling bacon filled the air. Annalee bustled about, serving plates piled high with scrambled eggs and crisp bacon.

"So, Mr. Galloway," Evelyn began, her eyes alight with curiosity, "what brings you to our little corner of Montana?"

Trent took a sip of coffee before answering. "Well, Miss Graham, I'm on the trail of some bank robbers who hit Helena not too long ago. Nasty bunch, but they've left quite a trail."

Faith leaned forward, her interest piqued. "You're a lawman, then?"

"Bounty hunter," Trent corrected, a hint of a drawl in his voice. "Used to be a Texas Ranger, though."

Faith's eyebrows shot up. "A Texas Ranger? How interesting."

Trent's eyes crinkled at the corners as he smiled. "It had its moments, Miss Goodell. I remember this one time in Amarillo…"

As Trent launched into a tale of a daring capture, Faith found herself hanging on every word. His voice painted vivid pictures of sunbaked prairies and dusty saloons, of desperate outlaws and narrow escapes.

"…and there I was, staring down the barrel of his gun," Trent continued. "I thought for sure my life was over."

"What happened next?" Annalee asked breathlessly, nearly forgetting the plate of biscuits in her hands.

Trent's grin widened. "Well, let's just say Lady Luck was on my side. A stray tumbleweed caught his eye for just a second, and that's all I needed."

As laughter rippled around the table, Faith couldn't help but notice the way Trent's eyes seemed to linger on her. She felt a blush creeping up her neck and quickly looked away.

"Mr. Galloway, you must have seen so much of the country in your travels," she said. "Have you ever considered writing about your experiences?"

Trent's eyebrows rose in surprise. "Can't say that I have, Miss Goodell. Why do you ask?"

"I run the Mystic Gazette. I'm always on the look-out for interesting stories. Your adventures would make for quite the serial."

"An intriguing idea," Trent mused, stroking his chin thoughtfully. "Though I'm not sure I have the writing talent to do the tales justice."

Faith leaned forward. "That's where I could help. We could collaborate. Your stories, my words. It could be quite the partnership."

As the words left her mouth, she realized how forward her comment sounded. She glanced around the table, catching Joshua's furrowed brow and feeling a twinge of guilt she couldn't quite explain.

Trent, however, seemed delighted by the suggestion. "Miss Goodell, I do believe you're onto something there. Perhaps we could discuss it further once I've wrapped up my current business?"

She nodded, trying to ignore the way her heart raced at the prospect. "A wonderful suggestion, Mr. Galloway."

As the conversation flowed around her, Faith found her mind wandering, filled with visions of adventure and the allure of the unknown. She barely noticed the concerned glances Joshua kept casting her way, too captivated by the charming stranger and the exciting possibilities he represented.

Joshua's gaze darted between Faith and Trent, his chest tightening with each shared smile and enthusiastic exchange. He'd known Faith since childhood, yet he'd never seen her quite so animated, so enthralled by someone's presence. The realization gnawed at him, a mixture of confusion and annoyance simmering beneath the surface.

Evelyn chimed in, her voice pulling Joshua from his brooding thoughts. "Faith and I are heading into Mystic this morning, Mr. Galloway. Perhaps you'd like to join us? We could show you around town."

Trent's eyes lit up at the invitation. "That's mighty kind of you, Miss Graham. I'd be honored to accompany such lovely ladies."

Joshua felt his jaw clench. He cleared his throat, forcing a casual tone as he looked at Evelyn. Before he spoke, Cody jumped in. "You sure that's wise, Evelyn? We don't know much about Mr. Galloway's business here."

Evelyn turned to Cody, her brow furrowing slightly. "I don't believe there's much he could do. After all, Faith and I always carry the guns your family gave us."

"Mr. Beckett's caution is understandable, Miss Graham." He looked at Cody. "I assure you, my only intention is to accompany these ladies to town."

Cody's gaze locked with Trent's, a silent challenge passing between them. "I need to ride to town myself. I'll tag along with you."

The bounty hunter's charm was evident, but there was a sharpness behind those eyes that set Cody on edge.

"Jupiter could use some exercise," Joshua found himself saying. "Mind if I ride alongside you folks into town?"

"Not at all," Cody said.

Evelyn nodded, a knowing smile playing at her lips. "We'd welcome your company, Joshua."

Heading outside, Joshua couldn't shake the feeling something important had shifted.

Chapter Ten

The cool morning air did little to calm the storm of emotions brewing within Joshua. He watched as Trent mounted his horse while Faith and Evelyn settled into the buggy.

With a tight grip on Jupiter's reins, Joshua swung into the saddle. A man always content to let life unfold around him felt an urgent need to take action, to make his feelings known before it was too late.

Cody rode up alongside the buggy, his gaze sweeping over Galloway, who had taken a position opposite him. As the small party set off toward Mystic, the Montana landscape stretched out before them. Joshua found himself acutely aware of every laugh, every shared glance between Faith and their mysterious new acquaintance. The road to town had never felt so long, nor so fraught with unspoken tension.

Joshua urged Jupiter forward, drawing even with Evelyn's buggy. He cleared his throat, searching for the right words to break the silence.

"Faith," he began, his voice softer than intended.

"I was wondering if you might have time later to discuss some ideas for the Gazette. There's been talk of some interesting developments at the ranch. They might make for a good story."

Faith shifted toward him. "Sounds intriguing, Josh. What sort of developments?"

Before Joshua could respond, Trent's deep voice cut through the air. "Speaking of interesting stories, did I mention the time I tracked an outlaw through the Badlands in the Dakotas for three weeks straight?"

Faith's attention shifted to the bounty hunter, her expression alight with fascination. "No, you didn't. Please, do tell us more, Mr. Galloway."

Joshua felt his chance slipping away, the words he longed to say dying on his lips. He watched as Faith leaned closer to Trent, hanging on his every word. The rolling hills of Mystic Valley seemed to mock him, a vast expanse of missed opportunities stretching out in all directions.

As the outskirts of Mystic came into sight, Joshua's plan to speak further with Faith evaporated. When they passed the first buildings, a commotion near the bank caught everyone's attention.

A group of men on horseback burst out of an alley, guns drawn and bandanas covering their faces. The air filled with shouts and the thunder of hooves as the town erupted into chaos.

Joshua's hand instinctively moved to his holster, his eyes locking with Faith's in a moment of shared alarm. "Get down!"

Faith dropped to the floor of the buggy, along with Evelyn, at Joshua's shouted command.

The turmoil on Mystic's main street erupted like a powder keg. Shots rang out, shattering the morning calm as the masked riders tore through town. Cody aimed his six-shooter at the outlaws, firing off several shots. One rider flew off the back of his horse, while another clutched his chest before slipping out of his saddle and onto the ground.

"Stay down!" Trent shouted at the same time Joshua maneuvered his horse between the riders and the women, shielding Faith and Evelyn with his broad frame.

"I've got them," Joshua called back, his voice calm, despite the mayhem. "You take care of those bandits!"

Trent spurred his horse forward, aiming his six-shooter and firing. Cody joined him, the two galloping after the riders. Cody caught sight of Sheriff Brodie Gaines emerging from his office, shotgun in hand. Their eyes met, a silent understanding passing between them.

"Cody!" Brodie shouted. "Flank 'em from the left!"

Cody veered his horse down a side alley. The pounding of hooves echoed off the buildings as he circled around, hoping to cut off the bandits' escape route.

Trent continued down the street before detouring down another alley, torn between the immediate threat and the gnawing fear for the women's safety.

Emerging back onto the main street, Trent found

himself face-to-face with one of the masked riders. Time seemed to slow as they sized each other up.

"Don't do it, mister," he warned, his gun aimed at the outlaw.

The man's eyes narrowed above his bandana. "You ain't got the guts, boy," he sneered.

Trent thought of the threat the man in front of him posed to the women. His hand moved like lightning, the crack of his six-shooter splitting the air. The bandit toppled from his saddle, clutching his shoulder.

As quickly as it had begun, the gunfight was over. The remaining outlaws, seeing their comrades fall, turned tail and fled. The thunder of retreating hooves faded into the distance, leaving behind a stunned silence.

Trent dismounted, his legs shaky with fading adrenaline. He scanned the street, searching for any additional signs of danger. Walking to the fallen bandit, he noted the wound to the man's shoulder. He kicked the man's gun away before helping him up and marching him toward the jail.

With no one inside, he grabbed the keys and locked the injured outlaw inside a cell. Ignoring the man's shouts, he stormed out of the jail. Relief washed over him when he spotted Joshua and the women emerging from inside the mercantile, their faces pale but resolute.

Touching Faith's arm, Joshua felt the weight of all his unspoken words pressing down on him. He took a step toward her, determined to reveal his heart, when the sheriff's voice cut through the air.

"Joshua! We need to organize a posse. Those bandits can't have gotten far." Brodie stood in the middle of the street with Cody beside him.

Even with the chaos, Joshua was glad to see the two men together. They'd been best friends before the deaths of Cody's wife and daughter. Brodie had never adjusted to Cody taking off to find the killers.

Joshua hesitated, torn between his duty and the yearning of his heart. Faith's gaze held his for a moment longer, a question in her eyes he couldn't answer. With a heavy sigh, he turned away, knowing once again, the moment had slipped through his fingers like sand.

As he strode toward the sheriff, Joshua's mind whirled with possibilities and regrets. Would he ever find the right time to tell Faith how he felt? And if he did, would it be too late?

Grayson Beckett stood on the front porch of the main house, his keen eyes surveying the land.

"Jolene," he called over his shoulder. "Best come see this. Looks like we've got company."

Jolene emerged from the house, wiping her hands on her apron. She squinted into the distance, spotting a lone rider approaching.

"Who is it?" she asked, moving to stand beside her husband.

Grayson's hand instinctively moved to the revolver at his hip. "I believe it's Josh." As the rider drew closer, his posture relaxed. "It's Josh, all right."

Joshua reined his horse to a stop in front of the house, dismounting with a grace that belied his exhaustion. His usually neat appearance was disheveled, his clothes covered in trail dust.

"Grayson, Jolene." He nodded to each of them, his voice hoarse. "We've got trouble."

Grayson's brow furrowed. "What kind of trouble?"

Joshua took a deep breath, his eyes clouded with worry. "Those bank robbers from Helena? They hit the bank in Mystic. We thought they were headed toward Bozeman until Cody spotted their tracks taking a wide turn south. Appears they're headed this way. Brodie, along with Cody and the posse, are close behind me, but..."

He trailed off, his gaze drifting to the vast expanse of land surrounding them. Grayson understood the unspoken concern. Wild Spirit Ranch was isolated and vulnerable.

Jolene's hand found Grayson's, squeezing it gently. "We've weathered worse." She gazed up at her husband. "How do you want to handle this?"

"We need to warn the family and hands, get everyone prepared. And..." Grayson hesitated, a flicker of something passing across his face. "You, Little Cody, Ma, and my sisters need to be ready to hide in the root cellar."

When Jolene opened her mouth to protest, Grayson stopped her with a stern look. "You have our baby to protect. Ma and my sisters should be with you, just in case the outlaws find you. They're as good with six-shooters and rifles as the men. They'll keep you safe. Go inside and warn them. Josh and I will notify the boys and our ranch hands."

As Jolene disappeared inside, the sound of approaching hoofbeats drew their attention. A cloud of dust on the horizon heralded the arrival of more riders, their identities yet unknown.

Grayson's hand tightened on his revolver. "Could be trouble's found us sooner than we thought," he muttered, his eyes narrowing as he tried to make out the approaching figures.

The tension in the air was palpable as the brothers braced themselves for whatever was coming their way, the peaceful evening now fraught with danger and uncertainty.

The approaching riders thundered closer, their silhouettes sharpening against the fading light. Joshua's keen eyes narrowed, recognizing the lead rider's gait. "It's Cody and the posse," he announced, tension easing from his shoulders.

Indeed, Cody Beckett rode at the front, his face set in grim determination. Next to him was Brodie. Behind them were several other men.

"Did you find their tracks?" Joshua asked.

Cody reined in his horse. "They're headed toward Black Canyon and Flatrock," he spat out, his voice rough with anger and fatigue. "We'll be lucky to get close to them once they hide back in the canyon."

Hearing the news, already knowing how difficult

it would be to hunt the outlaws in the twisting canyons, Joshua's thoughts returned to Faith. Maybe the reason she'd never expressed deeper feelings for him was because friendship was all she could offer. Her obvious attraction to Trent Galloway seemed to confirm this.

"What do you think, Josh?"

Cody's voice shook him from the depressing turn of his thoughts. "Sorry. Wasn't listening."

"What are the odds of locating the bandits in Black Canyon?" Trent Galloway asked.

"One or two men might be able to pass by the guards without being spotted, but not an entire posse. Unless the outlaws can climb the straight walls of the canyon, there's just one way in and one way out." Joshua paused for the information to sink in.

Of the older Beckett brothers, he'd been the only one interested in exploring the canyon when they were young. Joshua and a friend from Iron Angel Ranch would explore it whenever their chores were finished and the weather held out.

"You're saying we should wait them out?" Cody asked.

"I never found any other way out." Then Joshua had another thought. "Unless we drop in from the top." The men chuckled at the suggestion. "Or contact the commandant at Fort Ellis. Let those boys in blue raid Flatrock."

Chapter Eleven

It was late afternoon when Faith Goodell sat in her kitchen, eating warm beef stew. Her mind churned with restless thoughts, not tasting the meal she'd prepared.

"This won't do," she muttered, pushing away her half-empty bowl. She stood abruptly, her chair scraping against the worn wooden floor.

Her eyes darted to the clock on the mantle. Still early enough. Decision made, she strode to the coat rack by the door, donning her favorite coat.

The streets of Mystic were quieter than usual as Faith made her way to the Mystic Gazette office. The fading sunlight glinted off the newspaper's painted sign.

Inside, Faith lit the oil lamps, bathing her father's old desk in a welcoming glow. She settled into the familiar chair, pulling out a fresh sheet of paper, her favorite dip pen, and an inkwell.

Her pen scratched across the paper as she began to write. Pausing, she tapped the pen against her chin, wondering what her father would think of the Alliance. A wistful smile tugged at her lips. Faith guessed he would say she was stirring up trouble. Then again, he always encouraged her to question everything. She returned to the task, adding more points to her list.

The scratch of her pen and the occasional creak of the old building were the only sounds in the quiet office. Faith lost herself in the work, the restlessness plaguing her earlier gave way to a sense of purpose.

Finishing the last point, Faith leaned back in her chair, stretching her cramped fingers. She glanced at the clock, surprised to see how much time had passed. Night had settled in, and Faith knew she should head home. Yet, as she gathered her things, a nagging feeling tugged at her. Something about the empty streets and the frightening events of the day left her feeling unsettled.

She shook her head, trying to dispel the sensation. Stepping out into the cool night air, she locked the office behind her. Faith couldn't quite shake the feeling change was coming to Mystic, and not all of it might be welcome.

Her hand lingered on the doorknob of the Mystic Gazette, her mind drifting from the Women's Alliance to the events of the day. The bank robbery, Trent Galloway's sudden appearance, and Joshua's quiet strength all swirled in her thoughts like leaves caught in a whirlwind.

During the walk home, Faith found herself pondering the two men who had unexpectedly dominated her thoughts. Joshua, with his stable presence, had been a constant in her life for as long as she could remember. She'd loved him for years, though Faith had never admitted her feelings to him. She wondered if he felt the same.

Trent, with his rugged charm and tales of adventure, stirred something new and exciting within her. The two men were as the moon and the sun. Joshua, so rooted to the land, and Trent a tumbleweed in a storm.

The bounty hunter's stories echoed in her mind, tales of justice served and outlaws brought to heel. Faith's journalistic instincts tingled with possibility.

She quickened her pace toward home as a cool breeze rustled through the trees. As she rounded the corner onto her street, a shadow moved in the alley beside Jennings Mercantile. Faith's heart leaped into her throat, her earlier bravado evaporating like morning dew. She froze, eyes straining in the dim light.

"Hello?" she called, hating the tremor in her voice. "Is someone there?"

Silence answered her, broken only by the distant howl of a coyote. She mentally shook herself, trying to laugh off her fear. But the safety she'd always taken for granted suddenly seemed as fragile as spun sugar.

Rushing up the front steps and into the house, she locked the door behind her. Faith leaned her back against it, her thoughts swirling.

She glanced at her writing desk, where a blank sheet of paper waited invitingly. Even with the late hour, Faith felt a familiar itch in her fingers. There were stories to be told, and she was the one to tell them. Whether it was the Women's Alliance, Trent's adventures, or the changing face of Mystic itself, Faith knew one thing. Her pen would be busy in the days to come.

The following morning, Faith stepped out into the crisp Montana air, her folio tucked securely under her arm. As she strode toward the newspaper office, she spotted a familiar figure outside the sheriff's office.

Sheriff Brodie Gaines stood tall and imposing, his jet-black hair ruffled by the morning breeze. His eyes, usually twinkling with good humor, were clouded with concern as he gazed down the street.

"Morning, Sheriff," Faith called out, quickening her pace. "Did they catch the bank robbers?"

Brodie turned, his broad shoulders relaxing at the sight of her. "Good morning, Faith." He nodded, his voice deliberate and measured. "I was hoping to catch you. Got some information you might want for that paper of yours."

Faith's eyebrows shot up, her instincts instantly on alert. "What do you have?"

"I've sent word to Fort Ellis, requesting they send some troops to help us deal with those outlaws holed up in Black Canyon."

Faith's eyes widened. "Troops? Will they venture into Black Canyon?"

"I'm hopeful they will," Brodie replied, his eyes meeting hers steadily. "These bandits are dangerous. We were fortunate none of the townsfolk were shot during their escape yesterday. Going into Black Canyon is dangerous, especially with the few men in the posse. The cavalry plus the posse would have a better chance of penetrating their defenses."

Faith nodded, already considering the implications of heading into what Joshua called the viper's nest. "Do you think all the men in yesterday's posse will volunteer again?"

A flicker of uncertainty passed over Brodie's face. "That's the other thing," he said. "Trent Galloway's decided to ride out to Fort Ellis himself. Told me he wants to join up with the troops if they do ride into Black Canyon. He implied the posse wouldn't be necessary. If that's so, I'm all for it."

Faith felt a sudden tightness in her chest. "If he rides with the troops, when will he be back?"

Brodie shook his head. "I'm not sure he will be coming back. He told me, whether the troops ride out or not, he may not be returning to Mystic. Men like Trent are like tumbleweeds. They never stay in one place long."

Her high good spirits sank. She'd known Trent was a drifter. Still, she'd hoped he might stick around long enough to share his stories.

"I see." She fought to compose her voice. "Well, I suppose you're right. A man can't change his nature, after all."

Brodie studied her face, his expression softening. "You all right? Cody told me Galloway had agreed to tell you more of his tales for the newspaper. Must be disappointing."

She straightened her shoulders, lifting her chin. "You're right. I am disappointed. The townsfolk would've enjoyed his stories. I was thinking about asking Lilian to create illustrations to go with them."

As Faith and Brodie concluded their conversation, the jailhouse door creaked open. A man Faith had never seen before emerged, his presence catching her attention. Tall and wiry, with thick auburn hair and piercing golden-brown eyes, he presented an air of quiet confidence.

Brodie gestured toward the newcomer. "Faith, I'd like you to meet Nash Beaumont, our new deputy."

"Pleased to meet you, Deputy Beaumont," Faith said, extending her hand. "I'm Faith Goodell, editor of the Mystic Gazette."

His handshake was firm but not overbearing. "Ma'am," he replied, his voice low and measured.

"Nash has come to us from Laramie," the sheriff explained. "Figured with all the excitement lately, we could use an extra deputy."

She nodded, her curiosity far from satisfied. "I'm sure the townspeople would be interested in hearing more about our new deputy," she said, turning back to Nash. "Would you mind if I wrote an article about you for the newspaper?"

Nash shifted his weight, a flicker of hesitation

crossing his face. "Don't reckon there's much to tell, Miss Goodell. I'm a man doing his job, is all."

"Oh, I'm sure that's not true," she insisted. "Everyone has a story, Deputy Beaumont. And I'm certain the townsfolk would be interested in the man who'll be protecting them."

Nash glanced at Brodie, who gave a slight nod of encouragement. "I suppose if the sheriff thinks it's all right, I'd be happy to oblige."

"Wonderful," she said. "Perhaps we could meet later today? I promise not to take up too much of your time."

Nash touched the brim of his hat. "As you wish, Miss Goodell. I'll stop by the newspaper office when my duties allow."

As Faith bid farewell to both men, her high spirits returned. A new deputy, an impending military operation, and the lingering mystery of the bank robbers were all superb topics for the Gazette. Mystic was certainly brimming with activity, and she was determined to chronicle every moment of it.

The bell above the Mystic Gazette's door jingled, startling Faith from her concentration. She looked up from her desk, pen poised in her hand, to see Nash Beaumont's tall frame filling the doorway.

"Deputy Beaumont," she greeted, rising from her chair. "I'm glad you could make it."

Removing his hat, he revealed thick auburn hair to match his mustache. "Miss Goodell." He nodded. "I hope I'm not interrupting anything important."

She gestured to a chair across from her desk. "Not at all. Please, have a seat."

As Nash settled into the chair, Faith couldn't help but notice the way he scanned the room, his golden-brown eyes taking in every detail. It was the gaze of a man accustomed to assessing his surroundings.

"So, tell me about your journey to Mystic. What brought you here from Laramie?"

His lips quirked in a half-smile. "It's not much of a tale, I'm afraid. Saw the posting for a deputy position and decided it was time for a change of scenery."

"Surely, there's more to it than spotting a posting. What made you decide to be a deputy in the first place?"

His eyes grew distant for a moment. "I suppose you could say it runs in the family. My father was a Texas Ranger. I grew up hearing his stories and watching him serve the community. It seemed a natural path."

She found herself drawn into Nash's world, piecing together the experiences that had shaped this taciturn man.

Their conversation flowed, touching on Nash's time in Laramie, his impressions of Mystic, and his hopes for the future. Faith's pen danced across the page, capturing not only the facts but the essence of the man before her.

As the interview drew to a close, he cleared his throat. "Miss Goodell, I hope I haven't taken up too much of your time."

She glanced at the clock, surprised to see how much time had passed. "Not at all, Deputy. This has been most illuminating."

Standing, he reached for his hat. Fingering the brim, he met her gaze. "I don't suppose you'd care to talk more over supper? The Buffalo Run, perhaps?"

She hesitated for a moment, her thoughts briefly flitting to Joshua Beckett. But her instincts won out. "Sounds lovely. I'd be delighted to learn more about your travels."

Chapter Twelve

The almost full moon lit the streets of Mystic as Faith and Nash strolled toward her house. The evening air was brisk, carrying the scent of woodsmoke from the stoves and fireplaces inside the homes. She tucked a stray lock of hair behind her ear, her mind filled with the tales Nash had shared over supper.

"I must say, Deputy Beaumont, your adventures make Mystic seem quite quaint in comparison."

His lips curved into a small smile. "Every place has its own story, Miss Goodell. Mystic's just waiting for someone to tell it."

She smiled. "Well said."

They reached her porch, and Nash tipped his hat. "I reckon you'd do a fine job of it. Don't ever sell yourself short. There's a whole world out there waiting to be written about."

As he bid her goodnight and disappeared into the darkness, Faith found herself rooted to the spot, his words echoing in her mind. She sank onto the porch swing, the gentle creaking a counterpoint to her jumbled thoughts.

Mystic spread out before her, familiar and comforting. Yet Faith felt a restlessness stirring within her. She thought of Trent Galloway and Nash Beaumont, of the vast country beyond Mystic's borders, wondering if there was more out there for her. What if her story didn't end in Mystic?

As quickly as the thought arose, another followed. Joshua Beckett's face swam into her mind, his familiar presence an anchor in the sea of uncertainty.

"Oh, Joshua," she murmured. "Where do you fit in all this?"

The porch swing swayed, as if encouraging her musings. Her gaze drifted to the distant mountains, their peaks silhouetted against the star-studded sky. As the night deepened around her, she remained on the porch, her heart and mind grappling with the choices before her. The future, once so clear, now seemed as vast and mysterious as the Montana sky above.

A sudden gust of wind swept across the porch, rustling the papers Faith had brought home from the Gazette. One sheet caught the breeze, dancing out of her reach. As she lunged to grab it, a name caught her eye. "Flatrock."

Faith's breath caught in her throat. She snatched the paper, her eyes scanning the hastily scrawled notes she'd jotted down earlier in the day. In all the excitement of meeting Nash and the lingering thoughts of Joshua, this crucial piece of information had slipped her mind.

"Flatrock," she whispered, her heart racing. "The outlaws' hideout."

She stood and paced the porch, the floorboards creaking beneath her feet, considering her options. A horse nickered in the distance, and her head snapped up. An idea, dangerous and thrilling, began to take shape in her mind. She could ride out tonight, under the cover of darkness.

"It's madness," Faith told herself, even as she felt her resolve hardening. "Absolute madness."

Yet she found herself moving inside the house, her hand reaching for her heaviest coat. The night air seemed to whisper promises of adventure, of stories waiting to be told.

Rushing outside, she hurried toward the livery. Careful not to make any noise opening the gate, she approached the chestnut mare Josiah Jarvis always saddled for her. Seeing her approach, the horse nickered in greeting.

As her hands closed on the saddle, a shadow fell over her. She froze, her heart hammering in her chest. Slowly, she turned to face the unexpected visitor.

"Going somewhere, Faith?"

The shadowy figure stepped into the moonlight, revealing the stern countenance of Sheriff Brodie Gaines. His eyes, usually warm and friendly, now held a mixture of concern and suspicion.

Her hands dropped from the saddle, her pulse quickening. "Brodie," she managed, striving for a casual tone. "What brings you out so late?"

His gaze swept over her attire, lingering on the heavy coat, the one he knew she wore when it snowed. "I could ask you the same question. Seems to me you're fixin' to go on a late-night ride."

The cool night air swirled around them as the mare nickered once more. In the distance, a coyote's howl pierced the silence, adding to the tension of the moment.

Faith weighed her options. She could lie, make up some excuse, but the thought of deceiving Brodie sat ill with her. Taking a deep breath, she decided on honesty.

"I remembered something. Thought I might check it out myself."

His eyebrows shot up. "And it couldn't wait 'til morning?"

"It's about the robbers," Faith pressed on, her words tumbling out in a rush. "I understand they're holed up in Black Canyon. Probably in Flatrock." She glanced away, realizing how ridiculous her idea would sound.

"And?"

"And, well... I had the idea to ride out there and see if I might be able to find them. For a story, I mean."

Brodie's expression shifted, shock and anger crossing his features as his voice rose. "Flatrock? You were going to ride out alone to a town with a saloon, a house of ill repute, and a livery. A town brimming with outlaws to get a story?" The censure in his voice had her wincing.

"I guess it doesn't sound quite as sensible as it did when I first thought about it."

Brodie's eyes narrowed, his voice harsh as he took a menacing step toward her. "It's a darn fool notion, and you know it. Flatrock isn't safe during the day, and is darn right murderous at night."

As if to underscore his point, a sudden gust of wind rattled the livery railings, sending shadows dancing across the stables. Faith shivered, not entirely from the cold.

Brodie regarded her for a long moment, his expression unreadable. "Most of the time, your heart's in the right place, Faith, but your head isn't thinkin' straight tonight. Now, here's what you're gonna do..."

The sun crested the distant horizon when Faith found herself seated at her desk in the Mystic Gazette office, her fingers punching keys on her father's typewriter. The events of the previous night continued to weigh on her as she crafted her latest article, weaving together the facts of Nash Beaumont's experience with the story of his travels, ending with his arrival in Mystic.

A gentle knock at the door interrupted her focus. She looked up to see Nash Beaumont, the subject of her article, standing in the doorway with his hat in his hands.

"Mornin', Miss Goodell." A hint of a smile played

at the corners of his mouth. "Sheriff Gaines asked me to check in on you. Make sure you weren't planning any more midnight adventures."

She felt a flush creep up her neck. "Deputy Beaumont, I assure you, I've learned my lesson. My place is here, reporting the news, not gallivanting about in the dark."

Nash's smile widened. "Glad to hear it. Though I must admit, your spirit is admirable. Not many folks would've had the gumption to even consider such a thing."

As he spoke, Faith found herself studying the newcomer. Something in his easy manner put her at ease, cutting through the tension lingering in the air.

Nash reached into a pocket, drawing out a glove. "Mr. Jarvis brought this to the jail this morning. He didn't know where else to take it. The sheriff wondered if you might be missing one." He chuckled as he walked toward her and set the glove on the desk.

Her face flushed again. Clearing her throat, she reached out and picked it up. "Why, yes. This does look familiar. I removed my gloves to pick up the saddle..." Her voice drifted off.

"Understandable. It can be hard to cinch up a saddle with gloves."

"Yes. Quite right." Opening the drawer of her desk, she slid the glove into it.

"If you don't mind, I'd best get back to the jail and let Brodie know you're in your office."

"Thank you, Deputy."

Walking toward the door, he stopped, turning

toward her. "Oh, and the sheriff asked for you to stop by the jail and let him know if you have the inspiration to ride out at night in the future."

Clamping her jaw shut, Faith stopped herself from a response neither ladylike nor civil.

Joshua Beckett sat alone on the porch of the main house, a cup of coffee warming his hands before his mother called everyone to supper. His azure eyes were fixed on the horizon, where the sky met the jagged silhouette of the Rocky Mountains. His thoughts, however, were miles away, centered on one person. Faith Goodell.

He tried to think about the work waiting for him in the morning. Mending fences and moving cattle were never ending chores on the sprawling Wild Spirit Ranch. His mind should've been on them. Instead, it slipped back to the last time he'd seen Faith, after the bank robbery and his part in the posse tracking them.

Why was it so hard to tell her how he felt? He'd known Faith longer than anyone outside his family. She was as much a part of his life as the ranch itself. Telling her his feelings shouldn't be more difficult than confessing he preferred beef to chicken. Yet the thought of laying his heart bare made his hands go clammy, and his stomach twist into knots.

What if she didn't feel the same? Worse, what if

his admission put a strain on their lifelong friendship? He needed her in his life. Losing her would be unbearable.

Joshua remembered how devastated Faith had been after her father died, the deep hollows in her cheeks, the emptiness in her eyes. Joshua had been the one to convince her to keep the paper running, to persevere. He'd wanted to tell her everything would be okay, and he'd always be there for her. But fear had stopped him.

Confessing his love could change everything. It could mean losing her entirely. And yet, doing nothing might cost him even more.

Sipping his coffee, memories flooded his mind, unbidden, though welcome. He saw the two of them as children, running wild through the town of Mystic and up into the hills of his family's ranch. Faith had always been fearless, the one to dive into the swimming hole first or climb the highest branch of a tree. He'd been more cautious, following her wherever she led.

He thought of the time in high school when she'd been dating Ben Hadley. Joshua had simmered with jealousy, though he'd kept it well hidden. When Ben moved away and broke things off, Joshua had secretly been relieved, though he hurt for her all the same. She'd cried on his shoulder the night Ben left, and he'd been there, steadfast as an old oak in the following weeks.

More recently, he'd remembered the mid-summer evening she invited him to the newspaper's anniversary, celebrating ten years in Mystic. They'd eaten roast beef and potato salad, along with molasses cookies and wild blackberry tea. She'd told him stories of her parents and the early days of the Gazette. Joshua had been so proud of her, of everything she'd accomplished on her own.

Then there was last Christmas, when she'd come over to the Beckett house for supper. The ranch was snowbound, and she'd spent the night. They sat up late, drinking hot cocoa in front of the wood stove, talking about old times. He'd come perilously close to telling her then, the words "I love you" dancing on the edge of his tongue.

Every moment had carved her deeper into his heart.

The porch boards creaked as Joshua shifted in his seat, stretching his long legs. His mind was a tangle, a knot he couldn't hope to unravel. He wanted to tell Faith how much she meant to him, how he ached to be more than her friend.

He thought about Annalee, and how she'd been able to balance her friendships and her young loves. Joshua admired her, but he didn't share her fearless nature. At least not in matters of the heart.

Could he risk the life he knew for a chance at something greater? He wasn't sure. All he knew was he couldn't go on like this, with every interaction leaving him more conflicted, more unsure of where he stood.

He took another sip of coffee, now lukewarm. The horizon had shifted to deep oranges and purples, the sun slipping behind the mountains. Confession might ruin everything, but his silence was tearing him apart.

Chapter Thirteen

The rich aroma of Jolene's pot roast lingered in the air as Grayson savored the final bite, a taste hinting at home and comfort. With a contented sigh, he set down his fork, the clink against the plate echoing in the cozy kitchen. "You've outdone yourself again, Jolene. This meal might just fortify me for what lies ahead today."

Jolene's smile illuminated her features as she collected his empty plate, her eyes holding a depth of understanding. "Strength will be your ally, Gray. Sounds as if the town council is brewing up quite the storm lately."

He stood and stretched, groaning. "True enough. As a council member, it's my responsibility to talk sense into the others."

In his study, Grayson shuffled through a stack of papers on his desk. He found the document he was looking for—a neatly written proposal—and read it over one last time. The words were as firm and unyielding as the Montana landscape. He opposed the additional tax on businesses, advocating for donations and volunteer work instead. He slid the proposal into a leather folio and latched it shut.

From the window, he could see the expanse of Wild Spirit Ranch, some of the finest land in the territory. The Beckett family had carved this spread out of the wilderness, and every inch of it was steeped in their sweat and history. The thought of new taxes biting into their livelihood made his blood run hot.

"Gray," called a voice from the hallway. It was his younger brother, Joshua, tall and lean as a prairie wind. "You heading out soon?"

Grayson stepped into the hall, folder in hand. "About to. Why?"

Joshua scratched at a two-day beard. "Thought I might come along. Got some business in town."

"Business, huh? Wouldn't have anything to do with a certain newspaper editor, would it?"

Joshua's face broke into a sheepish grin. "Maybe. I'm certain Faith and her Women's Alliance will be at the meeting, given what's on the docket."

Grayson nodded. "Suit yourself. I'll be leaving shortly."

He strapped the holster holding his six-shooter around his hips. Sliding the gun out, he checked the chamber, then tucked it back into place.

The folio in his hand felt heavier than normal. The proposal was solid, but the council had been stubborn about insisting raising taxes was the only way to raise the money for the schoolhouse expansion.

He walked back to the kitchen, where Jolene

stood on tiptoes, stretching to put a mixing bowl on a high shelf. Grayson kissed her on the cheek. "Don't wait supper. This meeting may take a while."

She touched his arm, concern etching lines in her otherwise youthful face. "Just come home safe, Gray."

"Always do," he said, though they both knew it wasn't a promise he could keep.

In the yard, Joshua sat atop his horse and was holding the reins of Grayson's roan gelding. Grayson handed the leather folio to him as he mounted up.

The dirt trail from Wild Spirit Ranch to Mystic was well-worn, a familiar stretch of road connecting the Beckett clan to the growing town. Grayson and Joshua rode side by side, the rhythm of hooves sounded a deliberate heartbeat.

"Faith's in a tough spot, you know," Joshua said after a stretch of silence. "If the new taxes pass, it'll impact the smaller businesses the most."

Grayson shot his brother a look. "You think I don't know that? The ranch isn't the only thing I'm worried about, Josh. Every business in town is stretched thin. That's why my proposal has to pass."

"It may be a hard sell if the council's set on the taxes. They think it's the quickest solution."

"Quickest isn't always best. And sometimes, the easy way out costs more in the long run. They'll come around, you'll see."

Grayson was grateful Joshua let it go. He needed his focus on the task ahead, not on familial dissent. Though if he was honest, he valued Joshua's blunt comments. His brother had a way of reading people

Grayson sometimes lacked.

The landscape rolled by, a mosaic of varying orange colors. Tall grasses and scrub brush, the occasional stand of cottonwoods, all set against the distant mountains. A sharp wind cut through the valley, carrying with it the first hint of winter. Grayson pulled his coat tighter around his shoulders and thought of Jolene's welcome when he returned after the meeting.

They lapsed into silence again, each man lost in his own thoughts. The bond between them was strong, forged in the same crucible of hard work and shared loss.

They moved their horses into a trot as the first buildings of Mystic came into view, the air buzzing with the murmur of a waiting crowd.

The main street of Mystic was a hive of activity. Townsfolk milled about, chatting in clusters and filling the air with a discordant hum. Grayson and Joshua dismounted in front of the town hall, a modest two-story building used for a wide range of activities. They tied their horses to a rail and surveyed the scene.

"Looks like half the town's turned out," Joshua said, eyes scanning the crowd. "And not all of them in a friendly mood."

Grayson followed his brother's gaze. He could see the worried faces of shopkeepers, ranchers, and laborers. These were hardworking people, the backbone of Mystic, and many of them looked beleaguered. What caught his attention most, though, was a rather large group of women standing near the front of the crowd. The Mystic Women's Alliance.

"Looks like the Alliance is out in force," Joshua observed. "Think they'll make a ruckus?"

Grayson shrugged. "They've got every right to be here. Probably more than most."

Joshua arched a brow. "Thought you were unsure about the group Faith founded."

Grayson sighed. "I'm not against the group. Many of them are business owners or work in their family's shop or restaurant. We'll see what happens once the meeting starts."

"Gray," Joshua interrupted, his tone more serious as he nodded at someone in the crowd.

He followed the direction of Joshua's gaze, spotting a familiar face. An older woman, petite with graying brown hair pulled into a loose bun, stood at the periphery, observing the activity. Naomi Beckett, their indomitable mother.

"So, this is where she took off to before lunch," Joshua said.

"She never misses a meeting," Grayson said. "I hope she backs my proposal. Her word carries a lot of weight."

Joshua gave a noncommittal grunt. "Well, I'm going to say hello. You coming?"

"In a bit. I need to check something first."

Joshua started toward their mother, then hesitated. "Gray. Whatever happens, you know I'm with you, right?"

He looked at his brother, at the man he'd grown

into. Joshua wasn't a boy anymore, nor was he merely a younger version of Grayson. He was his own person, with his own ideas and loyalties.

"I know." He grinned. "Thank you."

Joshua held his gaze for a moment longer, then turned and weaved through the crowd toward his mother. Grayson watched him go before walking in the opposite direction.

He pulled the leather folder from inside his coat and opened it, glancing at the proposal. The words stared back at him, uncompromising. He closed the folder and looked around the crowd again, this time taking in individual faces. These were the people he was fighting for, the people who made Mystic a wonderful place to live.

He spotted Joshua standing with their mother and talking quietly. Their expressions were unreadable from this distance. Still, the sight gave him a small measure of hope. If his mother backed her son's proposal, it was as good as done.

Moving through the crowd, he entered the building along with the mayor and other members of the council. Taking their seats, Mayor Carl Jurgen nodded to a man who stood at the closed front door. Opening it, the people flowed inside, talking as they sat down.

The interior of the town hall was a stark contrast to the bustling street outside. Plain wooden benches lined the walls, with several other benches placed in the center of the room. At the table set up at the far side of the room sat the members of the Mystic town council, their faces set in various degrees of seriousness.

Grayson set the folio in front of him. He exchanged curt nods with the other council members. Doyle Shaw, owner of the general store, Pastor Owen Ward, Tripp Lassiter, a fellow rancher and friend of the Becketts, and Artemis Graham, president of the local bank. Casper Jennings, owner of Jennings Mercantile, leaned back in his chair with an air of studied indifference. At the center of the table sat Mayor Carl Jurgen, the owner of the lumberyard.

"Let's come to order," Jurgen said, tapping the table with his gavel. The room quieted, though a tense undercurrent remained. "First on the agenda is the proposal for new taxes on businesses to support the expansion of the schoolhouse. We'll open the floor to comments after the council has had a chance to speak."

Grayson noted the subtle shift in Jurgen's wording. Jurgen wasn't interested in an alternative to the proposed tax. He unclasped the folio and pulled out the proposal, holding it but making no move to pass it around.

"We all know times are tough," Jurgen continued. "The schoolhouse is too small for the number of children. The proposed tax is a modest one, but it could make a big difference. Councilman Beckett, you had some concerns?"

All eyes turned to Grayson. He cleared his throat, feeling the gaze of the crowd, as well as the scrutiny of his fellow council members.

"I do. No one disputes the need to support the school. But adding new taxes in an already difficult time will overly burden our businesses. We need to find a solution without imposing another tax on our hardworking citizens."

Casper Jennings leaned forward, no longer feigning his boredom. "And what solution do you suggest, Grayson? Cutting the school budget?"

"I suggest we look to the community for voluntary contributions. Donations would be used for materials, and volunteers would provide the labor. We can achieve the same goals without putting an additional burden on our shopkeepers and ranchers."

Artemis Graham let out a derisive snort. "You mean relying on charity. That's a fine idea in a church sermon, but we need something more reliable."

"Charity builds community, Artemis," Grayson shot back. "And it's every bit as reliable as the people of Mystic. Do you not have faith in your neighbors?"

Pastor Ward raised a hand, palm outward. "Let's not turn this into a theological debate. Grayson has a point. The question is whether enough people would step up."

"They will," Grayson said, with more conviction than he felt. "They always have. Remember when the mill shut down? We got through that because folks pitched in and helped each other. This is no different."

Tripp Lassiter tapped a pencil on the table, a gesture reminding Grayson of him and Tripp when they were in school. "It's a nice thought, Gray, and I support what you're saying. I'd be willing to volunteer my time and a few of my ranch hands for a day or two. But we're in different times as far as donations. People don't have much extra money these days."

"Which is exactly why a new tax would hurt more than help," Grayson said. "I'm not saying it's an easy fix. Guess we won't know about donations until we give it a try."

The crowd agreed with him, clapping and cheering at his words.

Mayor Jurgen tapped his gavel on the table again. "All right, now. Quiet down. We'll hear from the public now. Remember, we have two proposals."

Grayson suppressed a sigh of relief. Jurgen wasn't trying to railroad the issue. The mayor gestured to the crowd, and several hands shot up, including Faith Goodell's. Before Carl called on anyone, people began shouting their opinions. Finally, he banged the gavel loud enough to get everyone's attention.

Once the crowd settled down, Mayor Jurgen nodded at Faith, then pointed the gavel at her. "The floor is yours, Miss Goodell."

Chapter Fourteen

Joshua had made his way toward Faith, finding a seat right behind her. Grayson noted the two of them with a sense of unease. He liked Faith. She was smart, principled, and had a clear vision for the future of the town. Her newly created Women's Alliance added a layer of complication he didn't need right now.

Faith stood, looked around at the people she'd known her entire life, and smiled before turning back toward the council members. "First, I believe everyone here knows I have always supported the school and the education of our children," she said. "I will continue to support any measure that will keep them viable."

A murmur ran through the room, half approval, half apprehension.

"That said," she continued, "I believe in practical solutions. Councilman Beckett's proposal is indeed charitable. More importantly, it's realistic. Many of us remember how our mothers and fathers got by during the lean years. We helped each other. We didn't add to each other's burdens."

Grayson felt a pang of relief. If Faith and her Alliance threw their weight behind him, it could make all the difference.

"I believe you should know there are a great number of women and men who agree with the councilman's idea. We are the same people who would be willing to donate money and time to see it gets carried out as Grayson envisions."

Several men whistled while others cheered, and others began talking between each other. It took several minutes before Mayor Jurgen regained control.

"Thank you, Miss Goodell. We appreciate your opinion."

"And it's the opinion of the newly formed Mystic Women's Alliance. It will also appear in today's Gazette. I thought it only right everyone knew what the newspaper editor believes is the right approach. Thank you for hearing me out."

Faith sat down, and the room took a collective breath. She'd presented herself well while placing the onus on the council and indicating the Alliance's support.

Mayor Jurgen stroked his chin. "Your input is always valued, Miss Goodell." He looked as if he might say more, then shrugged. "Any other comments?"

Several hands went up, but the crowd's fervor had cooled. Grayson suspected many felt their concerns had already been voiced and answered, at least in part, by Faith. He eyed the time on his pocket watch. The meeting had stretched to an hour already.

One by one, the remaining hands trickled down, their owners unwilling to prolong the session with repetitive points. Grayson let out a slow breath, hoping Faith's words would sway the other councilmen.

"Very well," Jurgen said. "We appreciate everyone's—"

"Wait," came a voice from the center of the room. Grayson's heart sank as he recognized it. Strong and unyielding, it belonged to his mother, Naomi Beckett.

She stood, and the room tilted toward her like plants seeking sunlight.

"Naomi, you're more than welcome to add your thoughts," Jurgen said. "Just remember, no decision will be made today."

Naomi's eyes locked on Grayson, then moved to Joshua, then back to Grayson. "I just want to make sure we're all clear on what's at stake," she said. "And to add my support to Councilman Beckett's proposal."

Grayson relaxed at his mother's words.

"The school is more than a building," Naomi said. "It's the future of this town. Every child we educate is an investment in the future. We've always found ways to manage, and I believe we can again. The Becketts will volunteer time to help erect the addition to the schoolhouse, and I'm certain many of you at the table will be more than happy to supply donations of material." She pinned each one of the men with her hard glare. "Won't you, gentlemen?" Naomi sat back down, back straight and hands resting in her lap.

Mayor Jurgen set down his gavel, the wood clicking softly against the table. "The council will take all viewpoints into consideration," he said, his voice assuming a judicious tone. "We know these are difficult times, and no one takes this decision lightly."

Grayson suspected Jurgen had felt the shift in the room. What had seemed a foregone conclusion at the start of the meeting was now moving in the opposite direction. The locals had made their preference known.

"Thank you all for coming," Jurgen finished. "We'll reconvene next week to make a final decision. Meeting adjourned."

He tapped his gavel, and the room exploded into conversation. Grayson stayed seated, watching as the crowd filtered toward the door. He saw Joshua linger by Faith, saying something low and earnest. Whatever it was, she gave a slow nod, her face set in a dispassionate mask.

Grayson stood and stretched, his body stiff from the prolonged tension. He walked toward the door, where Joshua now stood alone, his eyes following Faith as she left.

"How'd she take it?" Grayson asked.

Joshua shrugged. "She knows it's out of her hands for now. She did what she came for, as did the women in the Alliance. Carl holding off the vote is concerning."

"I don't believe Carl is stalling. He's playing it safe

by allowing time for the other council members to think through what they heard today. Carl's not going to stand against Faith."

"Or Naomi Beckett." Joshua smiled.

Grayson placed a hand on his brother's shoulder. "Come on. Let's talk to Ma."

They took their time, letting the last of the crowd disperse. Outside, a chill bit through the air.

Naomi Beckett stood by the horses. "Well?" she asked as they approached.

"They listened," Grayson answered. "The crowd supported you and Faith. You made a significant impact."

Naomi nodded, her stern features softening a little. "You made a good case. Your father would be proud."

The knot in Grayson's stomach loosened at her words. He'd been waiting for her verdict, knowing her approval could be a bellwether for the community.

"Thanks, Ma."

She turned her sharp eyes on Joshua. "And you? Where do you stand in all this?"

Joshua met her gaze evenly. "I stand with my brother."

"Good," Naomi said. "The Becketts need to speak with one voice. I'll ride back with you, Grayson." She swung up into the saddle.

Grayson looked at Joshua. "Are you riding back now?" He mounted up, the leather creaking under his weight.

"I'm meeting Faith at the Golden Griddle. I'll see you at the ranch."

Joshua Beckett stepped into the Golden Griddle, the aroma of sizzling steaks and fresh coffee thick in the air. He scanned the crowded restaurant with the practiced ease of a rancher surveying a herd. Spotting Faith seated near the front window, he walked toward her. She looked up and waved.

"Hello, Josh." Her eyes shone with welcome.

"Faith."

"Have a seat. Maisy will be over to take our orders." She gestured to the chair next to her.

"Don't mind if I do. How'd you think the meeting went?"

She settled back into her chair. "Better than expected. Your brother did an excellent job presenting his idea."

"Grayson's had practice. The ranch is a handful, and now the council."

"He seems capable of dealing with both. Do you think his proposal will pass?"

Joshua rested his arms on the table. "Hard to say. The council is split, but Grayson can be persuasive."

Maisy appeared at their table. "What can I get you two?"

Placing their orders, Faith's gaze met Joshua's. "I'm learning it's a fine line between informing the public and stirring up trouble."

He looked at her for a long moment. "You walk it well."

"Thank you, Josh. Have you met the new deputy yet?"

"Not yet."

Faith looked past Joshua. "Well, there he is now."

Joshua turned to see a tall, broad-shouldered man with a thick auburn mustache entering the restaurant. He wore a tan duster and weathered Stetson. A tin star gleamed on his chest.

Faith lifted a hand and waved. The deputy's gaze landed on Faith. Removing his hat, he made his way over.

"Miss Goodell," Nash said. "I believe you're one of the Beckett boys. Brodie pointed you out to me at the council meeting."

"Joshua," Joshua said, rising to shake the man's hand.

"Your family's well-regarded around these parts."

Joshua sat back down, his eyes flicking to Faith. "You two know each other?" he asked.

Faith smiled. "We've crossed paths. Brodie introduced us."

"It's always good to get to know the editor of the local paper," Nash said.

Joshua noted the familiarity with which Faith and Nash interacted. It was a small town where everyone knew everyone else. Still, it gnawed at him.

"Care to join us?" Faith asked, gesturing to an empty chair. "We were just talking about the town council meeting."

"It'd be nice to have company." Nash pulled out the chair and took a seat.

Maisy brought out two plates filled with the day's special and set them down. "What can I get you, Deputy?"

"The same as they're having."

"I'll be right back," Maisy said, heading back to the kitchen.

Joshua took a deep breath, fighting the urge to take control of the conversation.

"Your brother seems to know his stuff," Nash said. "It's good to see some leadership in this town."

Faith leaned in, her posture open and engaged. "We're growing quickly, with all the problems of a larger town."

"Problems mean progress," Nash said, shrugging. "You can't have one without the other. It sure is an interesting time."

Joshua watched as Faith and Nash fell into an easy rhythm. It was supposed to be his time with her. He thought of all the words he'd planned to say and silently fumed.

They continued talking. Nash spoke of his experiences in Laramie, of the changes he'd seen, and of the balance between order and freedom. Joshua chimed in when he could, but it was clear Faith's curiosity was centered on Nash and his views.

Joshua's frustration simmered below the surface as the two seemed lost in their own private conversation. *Interesting times*, he thought, mimicking Nash's words. That's all it was to the new deputy, an observer playing his part. For Joshua, this was life. It was their ranch, their town, their future.

A future he'd thought would include Faith.

The three fell silent when Nash's supper arrived. When finished, he pushed his plate away, reached into a pocket, setting coins on the table before rising.

"I need to get back to the jail. Thanks for the conversation and the company."

Faith looked at Joshua, then back to Nash. "Of course. Enjoy your evening."

Joshua felt a brief, guilty relief. Maybe now he would have the chance he needed.

"Josh," Faith said, touching his arm. "Is something wrong?"

He turned to her, his eyes searching her face. How could he tell her what was really on his mind? Every moment he spent with her was torture and joy.

"I'm just tired," he lied. "It's been a long day."

Faith studied him, her journalist's eye not missing a single detail. He wondered if she could see the truth written on his face.

"All right," she said. "Are you ready to leave?"

More than ready, he thought. "Yes, I am."

They stepped outside, the cool evening air a stark contrast to the warm interior of the Golden Griddle. Nash was already some distance down the boardwalk, his silhouette tall and unyielding.

The walk to Faith's house was short. They didn't speak, the silence hanging heavy between them. He glanced at her several times, memorizing every detail.

When they arrived at her doorstep, Faith turned to Joshua. "Thank you for walking me. I could've managed, but it's nice to have the company."

Joshua stuffed his hands into the pockets of his coat. "It's no trouble. I enjoy our time together."

Faith hesitated, her hand on the doorknob. "Josh, if something is bothering you, you can tell me. We're friends, aren't we?"

Friends. The word struck him like a hammer blow.

"We are," he said, his voice softer than he intended. "I've got a lot on my mind. The ranch, the future."

She tilted her head, her long braid cascading to one side. "The future, huh? Sounds ominous."

"Faith," he started, then stopped. How could he phrase this so it didn't sound like a plea or a desperate grasp? "Do you ever think about leaving Mystic?"

She laughed. "Every day. But that's all it is. Thinking. Mystic is my home."

"Sure. But if you had the opportunity?"

"Why are you asking me this?"

Because I need to know where you see yourself. Because I want you to be a part of my future. Because I love you.

"The town is changing," he said instead. "Growing. Sometimes, it feels like we're being pulled along, whether we want it or not."

"Change is inevitable, Joshua. We can't stop it. Whether we want to or not, we'll have to adapt."

"I know. There are days I wonder if we're prepared for what's coming."

She released the doorknob and crossed her arms. "You're stalling. What is this really about?"

He looked away, down the street where Nash had disappeared. Maybe the deputy wasn't the real threat. Maybe it was the change Faith so readily embraced.

"It's about us," he said, bringing his gaze back to her.

She uncrossed her arms, her posture becoming less defensive, more open. "What about us?"

This was it. His heart thudded in his chest, each beat a ticking clock counting down to an uncertain future.

"Faith," he said. "I don't want to lose you."

Her eyes widened, and for a split second, he thought she might step into his arms. "Lose me? Josh, you're not going to—"

He took a deep breath, the cold air searing his lungs, and reached for her hand.

Chapter Fifteen

The explosion rocked Faith's front porch, splintering wood and rattling glass. She took a step back at the same time Joshua dropped his hand.

"Get inside!" he barked, his voice cutting through the stunned silence following the blast. She hesitated, eyes wide, then ducked through the front door as Joshua pulled his revolver from its holster. The weight of the iron was a familiar comfort in his hand.

He scanned the small town of Mystic, his gaze sharp as an eagle's. Townsfolk emerged from shops and homes, their faces masks of confusion and fear. A plume of smoke curled from the direction of the explosion.

Joshua's heart thudded in his chest. He thought of the people he'd come to care for, sending up a prayer no one had been hurt.

He took off at a dead run, boots pounding on the hardpack street. Energy surged through him, making the world around him feel both sharp and dreamlike.

The air was thick with dust as Joshua slowed,

taking in the scene. Sheriff Brodie Gaines stood with his hands on his hips. Beside him, Deputy Nash Beaumont shifted restlessly from foot to foot.

Joshua sidled up to the lawmen. He kept his revolver in hand, the barrel pointed at the ground but ready, as he surveyed the large hole in the bank's outside wall. "Heck of an opening."

"Looks worse than it is," Brodie said. "As far as we can tell, no one was hurt."

Nash squinted into the debris-covered bank interior. "Yet."

The hole in the wall was massive, a jagged maw exposing the building's insides. Smoke and dust wafted through the air. Joshua's eyes traced the outline of the breach, noting the splintered wood and brick. His gut tightened.

"Dynamite," Joshua said. "More than they needed."

Brodie grunted in agreement. "Darned fools could've brought the whole building down. We're lucky it held."

Joshua looked around, searching for faces in the growing crowd. "Any idea who's behind it?"

"Not yet," Brodie said. "But we'll find out. Artemus is checking the safe now."

The bank president had been in Mystic for years. He was a man who could be trusted, and was often called upon to help settle disputes between the locals.

Brodie turned to Nash. "You see anything?"

The deputy shook his head. "I was doing rounds. Heard the blast and came running. Must've just missed whoever did this."

Joshua took a step toward the ruined wall, peering inside. The bank's interior was in shambles, furniture overturned and papers strewn about. He saw the outline of a large iron safe against the back wall, the door open. Other than being covered in dust, it showed no damage. Artemus walked toward them, shaking his head.

"Most of the money is gone," he said to no one in particular. "I don't know how anyone could've blown the wall out, gotten into the safe, stolen the money, and ridden away before any of us got here."

"I arrived not more than a minute after the explosion," Brodie said.

Joshua walked around the perimeter of the bank, eyes scanning the ground for anything out of place. He spotted fragments of a wooden crate, the remnants of a fuse, boot prints in the dirt. His mind worked quickly, piecing together a rough picture of what may have happened.

"They knew there wouldn't be much time between the explosion and when you'd arrive, Brodie," Joshua said. "Could be the money was already waiting for them."

"What do you mean?" Artemus asked.

"Someone had the money packed up and ready to go. All the robbers had to do was get into the bank and take it."

"What are you saying, Beckett? You think one of my employees or I was in on this?" Artemus Graham looked around, once again assessing the scene, this time using Joshua's input.

Brodie stroked his chin. "It could've happened that way. Anyone know the combination other than you?"

Artemus looked at him, then sighed. "Just one person. But he's been with me since the bank opened." He didn't have to say more for them to know he referred to the head clerk, a rotund man with a restrained personality and cherubic face.

Joshua shrugged. "If someone's desperate enough, they can do almost anything."

Brodie turned to face him. "You're saying William Flock packed up the money for the robbers? If so, why the explosion?"

"Could be Mr. Flock already took the money with him. The explosion was theatrics."

Brodie nodded. "Guess I should find out if Flock is still in town."

The sound of a galloping horse drew the attention of the assembled townsfolk. A tall, lean figure dismounted with the ease of a man born to the saddle. Deputy Jubal Whitton tied off his horse and strode toward the bank, his face unreadable beneath the brim of his hat.

"Jubal," Brodie acknowledged. The deputy often patrolled the outskirts of town, a job he often took upon himself.

"What's the damage?" Jubal asked, his eyes taking in the scene with a slow, deliberate sweep.

"Big hole, lots of smoke," Brodie said. "No one hurt." He filled Jubal in on Joshua's theory.

Jubal nodded, then looked to Joshua. "Makes sense. Anyone check on Flock?"

"Not yet. I was about ready to head to Butterman's Boardinghouse," Brodie answered.

Jubal considered this, then spoke in his usual measured tones. "I'll check on him. Sure hope you're wrong, Beckett." Adjusting the gunbelt around his hips, he walked toward the boardinghouse.

Artemus watched the deputy leave, not offering to go with him. Instead, he headed back inside the bank.

The crowd had begun to disperse, the initial excitement giving way to wary resignation. In a town like Mystic, where life was often hard and unpredictable, the people were accustomed to occasional bursts of trouble. They returned to their daily routines, though Joshua noted more than one head turning back toward the bank with lingering concern. One familiar face caught his attention.

Joshua's heart skipped when he recognized Faith. She held a notepad in one hand, a pencil in the other, as she walked toward them.

"Brodie, Joshua," she said, nodding to each man in turn. Her eyes were bright, almost feverish. "What happened?"

Joshua opened his mouth to speak, but Brodie cut him off. "We don't know for certain, Faith. There are a lot of questions and few answers."

She frowned. "The town has a right to know. If there's a threat—"

"We'll handle it," Brodie said, his tone leaving no room for argument. "The last thing we need is panic."

Faith looked to Joshua, who shifted uncomfortably. He understood the sheriff's position, but he also knew Faith wouldn't be dissuaded so easily. Her father built the Mystic Gazette from nothing, and she continued his passion to find the truth and share it with the town.

"Brodie will tell you what he can, Faith," Joshua said. "Let him get the facts straight first."

Faith's eyes narrowed, but she held her tongue. "Fine," she said after a moment. "I'll wait." She stepped aside as the three men entered the bank.

The interior was a wreck, with bits of ceiling and wall strewn across the floor. Artemus Graham stood near the open safe. He held a ledger in one hand, clutching it as if it were a life preserver.

"Artemus," Brodie said. "Talk to us."

The bank president looked up, his face pale. "It's all here," he said, waving the ledger. "The accounts, the balances. Several thousand dollars, gone."

Joshua studied the man. Artemus had the look of a frightened rabbit, eyes darting between Brodie, Nash, and him. He wondered if the bank president was telling them everything.

The bank president muttered something, then turned back to the safe. The lawmen and Joshua made their way outside, where Faith still waited.

"Anything?" she asked.

Joshua started to speak, but a glare from Brodie silenced him. "Like Beckett said, I'll tell you what we can. Later."

The sheriff and his deputies walked off, leaving

Joshua with Faith. She looked up at him, expectancy written in the lines of her face. He sighed.

"Stay out of the bank, Faith. It's not safe."

She huffed. "I can take care of myself, Joshua."

"I know. But this is different."

She twirled the pencil in her fingers. "I just want to know what's going on. For the paper."

"For the town, you mean."

She smiled. "The paper is the town."

He rubbed the back of his neck, conflicted. "Talk to Brodie. He'll have to answer your questions. When he's ready."

"Why not just tell me yourself?"

Because he was torn between his duty to Brodie and his desire to help Faith. "Brodie's already made it clear he'll give you more details when he has them."

Straightening her back, she gave a curt nod. "All right."

She walked off, leaving Joshua to ponder the explosion, the empty safe, and the woman who was never far from his thoughts. He watched as Faith made her way down the street, the determination in her stride unmistakable.

Artemus Graham emerged from the bank, along with the two lawmen. Brodie stopped next to Joshua.

"Appears whoever robbed the bank got away with over three thousand dollars. Artemus can cover the loss, but I want to find the money."

Jubal rushed up. "Flock is gone. Clothes and everything. Rosamund Butter didn't know he'd left."

Artemus's shoulders sagged at the news. "I just

can't believe William was a part of this."

Even though no one else was around, Brodie lowered his voice. "Maybe he's not. His quick departure does make him look guilty."

"I understand." The beleaguered bank president stalked off.

"Joshua!" Faith's voice cut through his thoughts. She stood on the boardwalk in front of the general store, her notepad in hand. He sighed and walked over to her.

Excitement mingled with worry shone in her eyes. "Casper Jennings thinks the payroll for the ranch hands in the area was in the bank. Including your family's money."

"Faith." Joshua's voice indicated his frustration. He already realized the Beckett money was part of what was stolen. "You need to let the law handle this."

She stared at him, her expression a mix of hurt and defiance. "I'm not trying to play detective. But people need to know what's happening. If the bank fails—"

He held up a hand to stop her. "It isn't going to fail. Sometimes knowing too much makes things worse."

She was silent for a moment, weighing his words. "What aren't you telling me?"

When he didn't answer, she continued. "I saw you talking to Brodie. He must know more than he's saying."

"He's the sheriff," Joshua said. "I'm just a guest.

We need to trust the people in charge."

She took a step back, as if he'd slapped her. "You think I don't trust Brodie?"

"I think you want answers faster than they can be given. Sometimes, patience is—"

"Is what?" she shot back. "A virtue? You sound like my father."

"Maybe he was right."

She glared at him, the kind of glare that could melt glass, then turned on her heel and started to walk away. Joshua reached out, wanting to stop her, to apologize, then reconsidered. Sometimes leaving Faith to her own thoughts turned out to be for the best.

He watched as she made her way down the street, the determination in her stride now mingled with something heavier, more burdened. He respected her, admired her for the way she'd continued the Gazette on her own.

Joshua thought about what Brodie had said. About him telling Faith what he could when he could. He hoped it would be enough to satisfy her. His attention shifted to Brodie and his deputies. They were forming a posse, and he wanted to be a part of it. He looked back at Faith's retreating form.

She reached the corner and paused, turning back for a brief moment. Joshua thought she might wave or shout something. She simply stared. He couldn't read the look in her eyes from this distance, but he imagined it was the same mixture of hope and frustration he felt.

She disappeared around the bend, and Joshua's shoulders slumped.

Faith kept walking, not sure where she was headed. The hole in the bank's wall loomed large in her peripheral vision. An explosion like this didn't just disrupt a bank. It jolted through the entire community.

Halfway down the block, she stopped and looked back. Brodie, Nash, Jubal, and Joshua were talking again, their postures more relaxed. She considered going back, demanding the answers she knew they were withholding. But what would be the point? Maybe they didn't know anything more or have a suspicion of who might have robbed the bank.

Her eyes drifted to the horizon, where the mountains stood tall and unyielding. The moon was climbing higher, indicating it was much later than she thought.

She looked down at her notepad, flipping through the scribbles. Her instincts had kicked in from the moment of the explosion, but now a heavy fatigue set in. How many times had she been in this position, balancing the need for truth against the potential for harm? Too many to count, yet each instance felt as acute as the first.

It was then Faith realized she was entirely alone. The sense of isolation struck her odd, given the main street was close by. A tingling sense of danger washed over her, setting the hairs on her neck upright.

Before she could react, a rough hand clamped over her mouth, and a strong arm wrapped around her waist. She was yanked backward with such force her feet left the ground. She kicked and thrashed, trying to break free, but her assailant was too strong.

She was dragged into a dark alley. Faith managed to elbow her captor in the ribs, earning a grunt, but he only tightened the grip around her waist. In a swift, practiced motion, the assailant stuffed a handkerchief into her mouth, silencing her cries.

Panic set in as she took stock of her situation. The alley was narrow, the kind of place where sounds were swallowed whole. She recognized the back entrances to a few businesses, but no one was in sight. Her heart pounded in her chest, each beat a ticking clock counting down her last moments.

Her captor hoisted her up with ease, throwing her over the lap of a waiting rider. She struggled to lift her head, to see who was beneath the wide brimmed hat, but the rider's hand pushed her down, crushing her chest. The world tilted and swayed as the rider maneuvered the horse out of the alley and onto the street.

Faith's thoughts were a jumble, though one image stuck in her head. Joshua, his gaze following her down the street.

Chapter Sixteen

The rider guided the horse down a back street. Faith caught glimpses of the town she'd grown up in, and the people inside the buildings. The millinery with colorful hats in the window, the barber shop where old-timers swapped tales, the livery stable tended by Josiah Jarvis. All of it seemed surreal, a dream she was waking from too soon.

Ahead of them were two other riders, both men, checking the alleys as they rode past. Someone needed to stop them. But the streets remained eerily empty, the storefronts devoid of life. It was as if the whole town had shut down after the explosion. Meanwhile, her world was falling apart.

They neared the edge of town, and Faith's eyes widened with terror. Once they were in the open plains, her chances of escape dwindled to nothing. She tried to memorize the silhouettes of the men in front of them, the shape of their hats, and the lines of the horses, storing every detail in case she survived this. In case she could one day tell the story.

A shout rang out, cutting through the oppressive silence. The rider pulled on the reins, and Faith's body whiplashed, her head snapping up to see who'd called out.

It was Joshua. He stood in the middle of the street, revolver drawn, his silhouette stark against the rising moon. On either side of him were Brodie and Nash, their six-shooters aimed at the riders.

"Let her go!" Joshua commanded.

The riders hesitated, and Faith felt the horse shift its weight, ready to bolt. She knew Joshua was an excellent shot, but could he hit a moving target without striking her?

Joshua took a step closer, his eyes locked on the rider. "This is your only warning."

The rider slowly lifted Faith into the air, and she feared he planned to use her as a shield. Then she felt herself falling. She landed hard on the dirt, her left shoulder taking the brunt of the impact, pain exploding.

A gunshot fractured the air. Faith flinched, expecting to feel the hot kiss of a bullet, but it never came. She looked up to see the rider slumped sideways, clutching his upper arm. With what strength he had left, he kicked the horse's flanks and held onto the saddlehorn. He galloped out of town along with his companions.

Joshua rushed toward her as Brodie and Nash ran past them, guns firing.

"Faith!" He knelt down, his hands hovering, unsure where to touch. "Where are you hurt?"

She tried to speak, but the handkerchief was still lodged in her mouth. Joshua gently pulled it out, and she gasped for air, each breath a knife in her ribs.

"I'm okay," she lied. "My shoulder…"

He examined her with the care of a physician, noting the way she held her left arm. "Probably dislocated. We need to get you to Doc Wainwright."

He helped her stand, hearing her painful intake of breath. "Joshua, who… who were they?"

"I don't know."

She grabbed his hand with her good one. "Could they be the bank robbers?"

"Maybe. Probably. I'll let Brodie and his deputies sort it out."

She let those words sink in, knowing he was right. But it rankled. She knew turning off her natural curiosity was next to impossible. It was a curse as much as a calling.

He shot her a look she'd seen many times during their friendship. Sliding his left arm around her waist, she leaned into him.

They started to walk, her steps hesitant. She glanced back once, toward the horizon where the riders had disappeared, and wondered if they'd return to complete what they'd started. Faith didn't understand why they'd targeted her instead of riding out of town right after the explosion.

Faith's jaw clenched tight against the searing pain radiating from her left shoulder. She blinked rapidly, fighting back the tears threatening to spill over. She refused to cry.

"How are you doing?" he asked.

"I'm fine," she managed through gritted teeth, though her pale face and trembling hands betrayed her words.

Joshua's eyes clouded with concern as he studied Faith's ashen complexion. "No, you're not," he said, his voice barely above a whisper. "Your shoulder needs tending to."

She shook her head. "I can't let this slow me down. The Gazette—"

"The Gazette can wait," Joshua interrupted, his tone gentle but firm. "You need to see Doc Wainwright."

Faith released a sigh, the fight draining out of her. "I suppose you're right." She winced as another wave of pain washed over her.

Joshua tightened his hold around her, his presence reassuring.

She glanced up at Joshua, noting the quiet strength in his stance, the genuine concern etched across his features. A memory flashed through her mind—Joshua as a boy, always the peacemaker among his rowdy Beckett siblings, always there with a kind word or helping hand.

Faith couldn't turn off the worry she felt. How would she get the story out about the explosion and robbery if she was laid up? Her father had always said a newspaper's duty was to inform the public, no matter the cost.

"You're awful quiet," Joshua observed, breaking into her thoughts. "What's on your mind?"

Faith managed a weak smile. "I'm thinking about the article I need to write. There has been so much going on."

Joshua nodded, his expression thoughtful. "You're right. I doubt what Mystic is going through is much different from all growing towns."

Faith found herself drawing strength from Joshua, even as her shoulder throbbed mercilessly.

"Josh," she said. "I don't know what I'd do without you."

"I'm just doing what anyone would do."

Faith shook her head, wincing at the movement. "No, you're not. You're..." She trailed off, searching for the right words. "You're special, Josh. Always have been."

The air between them seemed to crackle with unspoken tension. He opened his mouth to respond, but before he could, a sharp cry of pain escaped her lips as she stumbled on a raised spot on the boardwalk.

"Easy there." His arm tightened around her waist to steady her. "We're almost to the clinic."

Nodding, she bit her lip against the fresh wave of agony.

They approached the weathered clapboard building housing the town clinic. As Joshua expected, it was closed. Reaching the clinic's porch, Joshua guided Faith to a spot where she could lean her undamaged shoulder against the doorframe.

"Rest here for a moment. I'm going to fetch the doctor. Will you be all right for a few minutes?"

"I'll be fine. Just... hurry back?"

Joshua's expression softened. "Fast as I can." He turned and sprinted toward Dr. Wainwright's house behind the clinic, his long strides eating up the distance.

Left alone, Faith leaned her head against the cool wood of the doorframe, her mind whirling. She couldn't shake the memory of Joshua's strong arm around her waist, the gentle timbre of his voice. When had her childhood friend become this dependable man who made her heart flutter?

The sound of rapid footsteps approaching drew Faith's attention. Dr. Caleb Wainwright, his brown hair slightly disheveled, came hurrying toward her with Joshua close behind. The doctor's dark eyes quickly assessed Faith's condition as he neared.

"Faith. Joshua tells me you've had quite the mishap. Let's get you inside and have a look, shall we?"

As the doctor opened the door, Joshua stepped closer to Faith, his brow furrowed with concern. "How are you holding up?"

She managed a weak smile. "I've been better, but I'll survive. Thank you for fetching the doctor so quickly."

"Josh, if you could assist her to the examination room, I'll gather what I need from the back."

Supporting Faith, they made their way inside. The scent of antiseptic and herbs filled the air. Though usually comforting, they now served to heighten her anxiety.

"Josh," Faith whispered as they walked, "I hope this doesn't interfere with my ability to write. Those who live in Mystic will want to know what happened at the bank."

Joshua's lips quirked into a half-smile. "Always the intrepid reporter, aren't you? Even with an injured shoulder, your first thought is your next story."

Faith felt a blush creep up her cheeks. "Well, someone has to keep this town informed. Speaking of which, did you notice anything unusual when we were coming here?"

Before Joshua could answer, the doctor appeared in the doorway of the examination room. "Right this way. Josh, if Faith doesn't mind, you can help me with this."

"I'd rather he stay, Doctor."

"Good," Wainwright said as he examined her left shoulder.

Faith and Joshua's eyes met for a brief moment. The intensity of his gaze made her breath catch, and she found herself wishing this moment of closeness could last a little longer. The moment was interrupted when Wainwright cleared his throat.

"Faith, it appears you've dislocated your shoulder. We'll need to reset it in order to ease the pain and prevent further complications."

She swallowed hard. "I suspected as much."

The doctor turned to Joshua, who was hovering nearby. "Josh, I'll need your assistance. Please stand on Miss Goodell's right side and provide support."

Joshua moved into position, his azure eyes filled with concern. "What do you need me to do?"

As the doctor explained the procedure, Faith's thoughts drifted to what was coming. She'd heard stories of shoulder relocations, and the thought of the impending pain made her stomach churn.

"Faith." Joshua leaned in close. "You're the strongest woman I know. This will be over before you know it."

His words, spoken so close to her ear, sent a shiver down her spine that had nothing to do with her injury. She met his gaze, drawing strength from the warmth and admiration she saw there.

"All right," Wainwright announced, positioning himself. "On the count of three, I'm going to manipulate your arm. It will be painful, but only for a moment. Are you ready?"

She nodded, gritting her teeth. "As I'll ever be."

"One... two..."

Before he reached three, he gave Faith's left arm a sharp, sudden tug. The pain was immediate and intense, causing her to cry out. Her vision blurred, and for a moment, she thought she might faint.

Then, as quickly as it had come, the worst of the pain subsided, leaving behind a dull ache. She blinked rapidly, aware of Joshua's strong hands steadying her, his touch both comforting and electrifying.

"There," the doctor said, sounding pleased. "The shoulder's back in place. How does it feel?"

She took a shaky breath, realizing the excruciating pain from before had indeed lessened. "Better," she managed, her voice hoarse. "Thank you."

As the initial shock wore off, she became acutely aware of Joshua's proximity, his hands still gently supporting her. Their eyes met, and something seemed to shift inside her. The air seemed charged with an unspoken intensity, leaving Faith feeling both exhilarated and terrified.

Anxious to leave and believing the worst was over, she slid from the examination table, sucked in a short breath, and fainted.

Chapter Seventeen

If Joshua hadn't been holding her, Faith would've dropped to the floor. Instead, he lifted her up and laid her back on the examination table. When she awoke a moment later, both the doctor and Joshua were staring down at her.

"What happened?"

"You fainted," Wainwright said. "I want you to stay down for a while. I'll check on you in a few minutes. Josh, perhaps we should give her a few minutes to collect herself."

"Of course. Faith, will you be all right?"

"I'll manage." She attempted a smile. As the men left the room, she closed her eyes, taking deep breaths to calm her rapid heartbeat.

In the waiting room, Joshua paced while Wainwright jotted down some notes. He glanced up, his brow furrowed. "Quite a night we're having, isn't it? First the bank robbery, now this."

Joshua's head snapped up. "You know about the robbery?"

"Hard not to, with all the commotion," Wainwright replied. He hesitated, then added, "Actually, I saw something peculiar after the explosion. A man who looked remarkably like William Flock running down the alley behind my office, carrying a satchel."

Joshua's eyes widened. "William Flock? Are you certain?"

"Well, I can't be entirely sure, but the resemblance was striking. I found it odd, given he's employed by Artemus Graham. I'd have thought he'd be running toward the bank, not away from it. Of course, I'm not one hundred percent certain it was him."

Who else could it be? Joshua thought. If Flock was involved, this could be bigger than they'd initially thought. He glanced toward the examination room, torn between his concern for Faith and the urgency of this new information.

"Doc," Joshua said. "I appreciate you sharing this. It could be vital to the investigation."

Wainwright nodded. "I hope it helps. Now, shall we check on our patient?"

Joshua's mind whirred with possibilities as Dr. Wainwright pushed open the examination room door. The significance of Flock's potential involvement weighed heavily on him, but his concern for Faith took precedence as he followed the doctor inside.

She sat on the edge of the examination table, her face pale but determined. The doctor approached her with a gentle smile. "How are you feeling?"

"Better, thank you." Her voice didn't waver, despite the lingering pain evident in her eyes.

Joshua watched as Wainwright slipped on a sling to keep her arm stable, then helped Faith off the table. His hands steadied her as she found her footing. The doctor's movements were practiced and efficient, a testament to his years of training at Harvard Medical School.

"I'll walk you out," Wainwright offered, guiding her to the door where Joshua waited.

"Thank you, Doctor. I'm so glad you were available to fix my shoulder."

He smiled. "It was my pleasure. For a few days, wear the sling when you walk. Be careful with your shoulder for at least a week."

"All right."

When Faith stopped beside him, Joshua saw the strength in her eyes, the unwavering spirit that had drawn him to her since childhood. "I'll take you home," he said softly.

"I want to go to the newspaper office."

"But—"

"I'm fine, Joshua," she interrupted. "If you don't want to go, I'll walk by myself."

"You're stubborn. I'll give you that." Joshua ushered her outside.

As they stepped out onto the boardwalk, Joshua's mind returned to the pressing matter at hand.

"Faith," he began, his voice low and urgent, "I need to speak with Sheriff Brodie. It's about the robbery."

Her journalistic instincts spiked. "What about it?"

He hesitated, torn between his desire to protect her and his respect for her independence. "Dr. Wainwright saw something... someone. It could be important."

"I should come with you," she insisted.

He shook his head. "No, you need to rest. I'll fill you in later, I promise."

As they reached the door of the Mystic Gazette, Joshua's hand lingered on Faith's arm. The touch sent a familiar warmth through him, a reminder of the unspoken connection they shared.

"I'll be back in a while to walk you home," he murmured, his eyes conveying more than words could express.

With a final glance at Faith, he turned and strode toward the sheriff's office, his mind already formulating how to relay Dr. Wainwright's crucial information to Sheriff Brodie.

Faith watched his retreating figure for a moment, her mind wrestling with possibilities. The pain in her shoulder had dulled to a persistent ache, but her curiosity burned even stronger. She pushed open the door to the Mystic Gazette and stepped inside.

"I can't just sit idle," Faith muttered to herself, making her way to her desk. Removing the sling, she slid a fresh sheet of paper into the typewriter, her fingers itching to put words to the page. The explosion, the robbery, and whatever Joshua hadn't shared with her. It all needed to be told.

As she continued to type, the door creaked open. Joshua stepped inside, grabbed the only other chair in the office, and sat down.

"You must be exhausted. How about I walk you home?"

Faith's chin rose. "I'm almost finished with the piece on the explosion and robbery. It would be nice to end with whatever you had to tell Brodie."

Joshua leaned closer, his voice gentle but firm. "It would make a good ending to your story, but I promised Brodie not to say a word to anyone else. Including you. Think about what could happen if publishing this information jeopardizes Sheriff Brodie's investigation."

Faith's brow furrowed. "But surely the townsfolk should know—"

"Timing is crucial," he interrupted. "Why don't you wait for Brodie? Get all the facts before you print anything. You don't want to rush forward without all the facts."

She leaned back in her chair, conflicted. Her instincts as a reporter warred with the logic of Joshua's words. She studied his face, seeing the sincerity there.

"You're right," she conceded after a long moment. "I'll wait to speak with Brodie. But I won't sit on this story for long, Joshua."

His shoulders relaxed. "That's all I ask. We'll go

together to see Brodie as soon as he's available. Which will be after you get some rest."

"I am pretty tired." She slid the sling on, adjusting it to accommodate her arm.

Standing, he held out his hand. "I'm walking you home."

"Joshua?" He paused to look at her. "Thank you... for watching out for me."

A small smile played on Joshua's lips. "Always," he replied before taking her hand.

Joshua's hand hesitated on the doorknob, his heart pounding in his chest. The almost full moon streamed through the newspaper office windows, washing Faith in an ethereal glow. He swallowed hard, knowing if he didn't speak now, he might never find the courage again.

"Faith." He turned to face her. "There's something else I need to tell you."

"What is it, Joshua?"

He took a deep breath. "I've been wanting to say this for a long time."

Her eyebrows rose slightly. "Go on," she encouraged softly.

Joshua's usual quiet manner gave way to a storm of emotions. "Faith, I... I care for you. Deeply. More than just a friend. I think I always have."

The room fell silent, save for the ticking of the clock on the wall. Her lips parted in surprise. She stood frozen as she processed his words.

He waited, his heart in his throat, the tension in the room palpable. He could see the wheels turning behind her eyes. The silence stretched on, becoming almost unbearable.

"We should go," he finally said, his voice rough with emotion. "I'm sorry if I've made you uncomfortable. I just needed you to know." Opening the door, he motioned for her to walk past him.

He walked beside her, the quiet almost painful. Faith's unspoken response hung in the air like a phantom, creating a wall of unresolved emotions and possibilities.

The eerily quiet streets of Mystic seemed to echo with the weight of his confession as they made their way to her house. Walking up the steps, she opened the front door, not looking at him. He bid her goodnight, hesitated a moment, then hurried off.

She stood at the living room window, watching his figure disappear down the street. Her heart pounded against her ribs. She pressed her palm against the cool glass, her breath fogging the pane.

"Oh, Joshua," she whispered, her voice barely audible.

Chapter Eighteen

Faith woke with a start, the dull throb in her left shoulder immediately yanking her from the comforting fog of sleep. She blinked at the morning light filtering through the lace curtains of her bedroom, then tried to stretch, only to wince and bite her lip. The sling on the bedside chair was a stark reminder of the previous night's chaos. The rough hands dragging her from the street, of Joshua's timely rescue, and of his unexpected confession.

"Faith, you mean more to me than just a friend."

She sat up slowly, her good hand pushing against the feather mattress. Her head swam with a thousand thoughts, none of them bringing the clarity she needed. Did she love Joshua the way he loved her? The way he claimed to, anyway. Their friendship had always been the one constant in her tumultuous life. Was she ready to risk it for something more?

Slipping into the sling, her fingers traced the fabric, remembering how Joshua had gently adjusted it for her, his hands sure, despite the storm in his eyes.

He'd saved her, yes. Now, she felt more endangered than ever. Not for her life, but by her own heart.

She swung her legs over the side of the bed and stood. The room tilted. Catching herself on the bedpost, she took a moment to calm her breathing. The ache in her shoulder was nothing compared to the gnawing uncertainty in her chest.

Slowly, she crossed to the vanity and looked at the woman in the mirror. Dark circles smudged beneath her eyes, and her hair was a wild tangle of blonde vines. She ran a brush through it, then shrugged. No amount of grooming could tame the hurricane of emotions whirling inside her.

Walking across the room, she opened her wardrobe with her good hand and surveyed the contents. Each dress and blouse was a memory—of her father, of her growing up, of the times she and Joshua had spent together.

Chiding herself for putting it on before dressing, she removed the sling. She pulled out a simple dark blue dress and slipped it on, the motion awkward with her injured shoulder. The fabric was soft and familiar, like an old friend. Like Joshua.

Her mind drifted to the future. Could she really see them as a couple? Walking hand in hand through Mystic, sharing kisses behind the livery, stealing moments in the very kitchen where she now sat alone? Yes, she decided, she could. It all seemed so idyllic, yet so terrifyingly real.

Then there was the ranch. The Becketts had always supported her, taking her in when her house grew too lonely, and she needed to be around friends. If things went wrong with Joshua, where would the loss leave her?

She bit her lip, a habit she'd never quite shaken, and remembered the spark she'd felt when Joshua held her close after the ordeal. It wasn't just gratitude. It was something more. A great deal more.

With a sigh, she walked to the window. The town of Mystic was waking, the first tendrils of smoke rising from chimneys, the faint sounds of activity trickling in on the cool morning air. This was her world, her life, and Joshua had been at the center of it for as long as she could remember.

Turning from the window, she returned to the vanity, where a small photograph sat in a silver frame. Taken by Molly Beckett, it was of her and Joshua at the ranch, both of them grinning like fools. It was only two months ago, yet now it seemed a lifetime.

Taking the photo in her hand, she traced their faces with a fingertip. How easy things had been then, how simple. She longed for that simplicity, for the untroubled camaraderie they once had.

Setting the photo down gently, as if afraid to break the fragile memory it held, she picked up the sling. Her left shoulder throbbed in time with her pulse, each beat a reminder of her vulnerability. She didn't like feeling helpless, and she didn't like being in debt, not even to Joshua. Even so, here she was, owing him her life and so much more.

Slipping the sling over her shoulder, she winced

again and took a deep breath. The day stretched out before her, full of uncertainties and decisions she wasn't ready to make.

The rumbling in her stomach reminded Faith to eat breakfast before leaving for the newspaper office. Heading downstairs, she stoked the kitchen's cooling stove. She set a cast iron skillet on it before fixing coffee. Within minutes, the stove radiated enough warmth to heat the room.

Faith sat at her kitchen table, the wood stove battling the morning chill. A plate of eggs and a cup of coffee steamed in front of her, but she only picked at the food. The quiet of the house seeped into her bones, providing a comforting moment of reflection.

She remembered the first time she and Joshua met. It had been in the schoolhouse soon after Faith turned six. Joshua had been seven, with a broad smile and kind nature. He'd protected her when an older boy tried to steal her lunch.

From then on, he'd taken her under his wing, teaching her to ride and, eventually, how to shoot. They were inseparable, like brother and sister, except now she had to wonder if he'd always seen their friendship as something more.

Her eyes drifted to the small bookshelf in the corner of the kitchen. On the top shelf sat a book Joshua had given her for her twelfth birthday. *Little Women* by Louisa May Alcott had consumed all of Faith's time. What she loved the most was his inscription on the inside cover.

*For Faith, my very best friend. Joshua Beck-
ett.*

Now, she saw the gesture in a different light. How many other signs had she missed?

The eggs grew cold, the coffee lukewarm, as she turned these thoughts over and over in her mind. Outside, the sun struggled to make headway against a leaden sky, and light snow began to fall, its flakes dancing on the wind.

With a slow, deliberate motion, she cleared her plate and cup, then put on her heavy wool coat, hat, and gloves. She glanced around the kitchen, taking in every detail, as if committing it to memory. Home had always been a sanctuary for her, but the events of last night had shaken her sense of safety.

Faith stepped out of her house, the crisp autumn air nipping at her cheeks. The snow had stopped, though the biting chill remained. Her eyes darted left and right, scanning the quiet street of Mystic. The sling on her left arm felt like a constant reminder of the recent ordeal, and her heart quickened as she caught sight of a shadow moving behind a nearby tree.

Faith reminded herself she had to be careful. The outlaws who'd tried to kidnap her were still out there. Mystic was a small town with limited resources. Until they were caught, she needed to stay vigilant.

"Stay calm," she whispered to herself, her free hand instinctively reaching for the small Derringer hidden in her skirt pocket. The weight of the weapon provided little comfort as she began her walk toward the Mystic Gazette office.

Every step felt calculated, her senses heightened to an almost painful degree. The familiar sounds now seemed ominous and foreign.

As she passed Jennings Mercantile & Dry Goods. Casper Jennings glanced up as he swept the boardwalk. "Mornin', Faith. Heard about what happened. How's your arm?"

She forced a smile. "On the mend, Mr. Jennings. Thank you for asking."

"You take care now," he replied, his brow furrowing with concern.

She quickened her pace, her mind torn between the lingering fear from the kidnapping attempt and the memory of Joshua's confession. *'I love you, Faith.'* The words echoed in her mind, bringing a flush to her cheeks.

As she approached the bank, the sight of the boarded-up hole from the explosion stopped her in her tracks. Debris had been cleared away, leaving only a few stray splinters scattered on the ground.

A hand-painted sign hung proudly on the front door. "Mystic Bank. Open for Business."

Faith's lips curved into a small smile at the resiliency of her small town. The moment was short-lived as she caught sight of Sheriff Brodie Gaines approaching, his face grim.

"Faith," he greeted, tipping his hat. "How are you faring?"

Straightening her shoulders, she met his gaze.

"I'm managing. Any news on the outlaws?"

His gaze darted to the boarded-up hole before returning to Faith. "Not so far."

She nodded, her journalist's instincts taking over. "And the bank? Will it be secure enough until proper repairs can be made?"

"Mr. Graham has men working 'round the clock," he assured her. Glancing around, he fixed his gaze on her. "I'd feel better if you'd consider staying with someone for a few days. Maybe the Becketts—"

"I appreciate your concern," she interrupted. "But I'm going to stay in town. I have a newspaper to run, and I'm going to focus on getting the next issue printed."

"You're one stubborn woman. Promise me you'll stay alert?"

"Of course," she replied, her hand brushing against the hidden Derringer.

"I need to ride out to the Beckett ranch. Take care, Faith."

As Brodie walked away, Faith turned back to the bank, her eyes tracing the jagged edges of the boarded-up hole. With a deep breath, she continued her walk to the Gazette office, her steps more purposeful now.

The town of Mystic had weathered this storm, and so would she. Joshua's confession was a storm of a different kind, one she'd spend a good deal of time reflecting on.

Joshua Beckett took a swallow from his canteen, his eyes squinting against the late morning sun. The barn's roof had taken a beating during the last storm, and winter was coming on fast. He hammered another nail into place, the rhythmic sound echoing across the sprawling ranch.

"Jupiter," he called down to his dapple-gray Quarter Horse, who stood in the corral below. "Reckon I'll have this done before sundown?"

The gelding nickered softly in response, and Joshua chuckled. "Yeah, I thought so, too."

As he worked, his mind drifted to Faith. The memory of her face when he'd confessed his feelings was imprinted on his mind. Had he made a mistake? The friendship they'd shared since childhood was precious to him, and the thought of losing it twisted his gut worse than any wild mustang ever had.

"Darn fool," he muttered to himself, driving another nail with perhaps more force than necessary.

Even as doubt gnawed at him, Joshua couldn't bring himself to regret his words. Faith was strong-willed and curious, with a heart as big as Montana itself. He'd been in love with her for longer than he cared to admit, even to himself.

A sudden gust of wind caught him off guard, nearly sending him sliding off the roof. Joshua caught himself, his heart pounding.

"Focus, Beckett," he breathed. "Won't do Faith

any good if you break your neck falling off a barn roof."

As he resumed his work, Joshua's thoughts turned to the recent troubles in Mystic. His jaw clenched at the memory of the botched kidnapping attempt. If anything had happened to her...

The sun inched across the sky as he continued to work, his muscles aching but his resolve strengthening with each passing moment. Whatever came next with Faith, with the outlaws, he'd face it. After all, the Becketts didn't back down from a challenge.

Chapter Nineteen

Joshua wiped the sweat from his brow, his eyes scanning the horizon as he thought of Faith.

"What if I've gone and ruined everything?" he muttered.

The soft thud of approaching hoofbeats caught his attention. He turned, squinting against the sun, to see two familiar figures approaching on horseback.

"Brodie," he called out, climbing down from the roof. "Beaumont. What brings you two out this way?"

The sheriff dismounted, his eyes sharp beneath the brim of his hat. "Joshua." He nodded, his voice deliberate. "Got some news. Your family around?"

A knot formed in Joshua's stomach. "Most of them. Everything all right?"

Nash Beaumont, still astride his horse, scanned the area. "Best gather everyone, Josh. Sheriff's got some important information to share." He slid to the ground, his gaze still watchful.

"I'll call them out." He walked toward the main house, calling out, his voice carrying across the yard.

"Grayson! Cody! Everyone, come on out. Brodie's here!"

As the Becketts emerged from various corners of the ranch, Joshua couldn't help wondering if this visit had anything to do with Faith. Was she in trouble again?

Grayson, ever the protective oldest brother, was the first to reach them. "What's this about, Brodie?"

Joshua studied the sheriff's face, searching for any clue. Brodie's expression remained impassive, but there was a tension in his broad shoulders.

"Let's wait 'til everyone's here," Brodie replied, his voice low. "This concerns all of you."

As the rest of the family gathered around, a heavy silence fell over the group. Joshua's gaze flickered between his siblings, noting their worried expressions.

"All right, Brodie," Cody said. "We're all here. What's got you riding out here near the end of the day?"

Brodie took a deep breath, his gaze meeting each of the Becketts' in turn. "There's been a development with the outlaws," he began, his words measured. "And I'm afraid it might involve your ranch."

Joshua's breath caught in his throat. He glanced at Grayson, seeing his own fear reflected in his brother's eyes.

Brodie's voice was tinged with a mix of frustration and resignation. "We've been tracking the outlaws for almost twenty-four hours now. They appear to be riding north toward Helena." Resting his hands on his hips, he shook his head. "I'm afraid we've lost the trail."

Joshua's brow furrowed. "What do you mean? Surely, there must be some trail to follow."

The sheriff's piercing gaze reflected the weight of his responsibility. "That's just it, Joshua. These men are like ghosts. The posse searched between Mystic and Bozeman, then combed through Gallatin Canyon. It's as if they've vanished into thin air."

Grayson stepped forward, his voice tight with concern. "Are you saying there's nothing more to be done?"

Brodie's jaw clenched. "I'm saying, we're doing everything we can with what we've got. But the truth is, our resources are stretched thin. We can't abandon the safety of Mystic to chase shadows across the territory."

Annalee listened as Brodie spoke, and as always happened, she found herself drawn to his presence. To his strength and giving nature. She watched him intently, noting the way his broad shoulders tensed with each word, the furrow in his brow deepening as he explained the challenges they faced. Her heart ached to see him so burdened.

"Is there anything else we can do?" Annalee asked. "Maybe we could organize a search party, or—"

"It's too dangerous," Brodie cut her off, his tone gentler than before. "Your offer is generous, but I can't risk civilian lives on a search this dangerous."

Annalee's cheeks flushed, and she ducked her

head, hoping no one had noticed. But someone had. Joshua caught the exchange, a flicker of understanding passing across his face.

"So, what happens now?" Joshua pressed, trying to refocus the conversation.

"We keep our eyes and ears open. Double patrols around town and the surrounding ranches. And I'm asking all of you to stay vigilant. Report anything suspicious, no matter how small it might seem."

As the family absorbed this news, Joshua noticed the subtle shifts in their demeanor. Cody's jaw muscles twitched while Grayson's hands flexed at his sides. Nathan's gaze darted to the distant hills, as if expecting trouble to come riding over them at any moment.

But it was Annalee who held Joshua's attention. She hadn't taken her eyes off Brodie, her gaze a mix of admiration and worry. He watched as she took a small step closer to the sheriff, her voice barely above a whisper.

"You're doing everything you can, Brodie. We all see that."

Brodie's eyes softened as they met Annalee's, a ghost of a smile touching his lips. "I appreciate that, Annie. More than you know."

The moment stretched between them, charged with unspoken emotions. Joshua glanced at his mother, wondering if she noticed the exchange. His mother's knowing smile told him she had.

"We'll do whatever it takes to keep Mystic safe," Joshua declared. "You have our word on that,

Brodie."

"I know I can count on the Becketts. Always have."

As Brodie and Nash prepared to mount their horses, Joshua stepped forward, his azure eyes glinting with resolve. "Mind if I ride along with you fellas?"

Brodie nodded, a hint of understanding in his expression. "Sure thing, Joshua. We'd welcome the company."

Joshua turned to his family. "I'll be back before sundown."

Heading toward the barn to saddle Jupiter, he considered the best way to approach Faith about the confession he'd made.

"You ready, Josh?" Brodie's voice echoed from outside.

"Coming," he called back, leading Jupiter out into the yard.

As he swung into the saddle, Joshua couldn't help but notice the knowing looks exchanged between his siblings. Nathan's smirk, in particular, rankled him.

"Something amusing?" Joshua asked, his tone light despite the nervousness churning in his gut.

Nathan chuckled. "Just wondering if you'd pick up the latest edition of the Gazette while you're in town."

Not willing to be dragged into mentioning Faith, he shrugged. "Be happy to."

As the three men rode away, his thoughts drifted to a certain woman with green eyes, blonde hair, and a stubborn character stronger than most men he knew.

"You seem distracted," Brodie observed, breaking the silence. "Something bothering you?"

Joshua forced a smile. "Nothing important. Let's pick up the pace."

The three men urged their horses forward, the uncertainty of what lay ahead spurring them on.

When they entered Mystic, the late afternoon activity of the town enveloped them. The familiar sights and sounds filled Joshua's senses as his gaze darted toward the newspaper office.

"I'll be heading to the jail," Brodie announced, reining in his horse. "Josh, if you have time, stop by before you leave town."

"Will do."

Parting ways, Joshua's anticipation grew. He guided his horse down the street, his heart pounding when he spotted Faith through the front window of the Gazette office. As he dismounted, a commotion erupted from the Starlight Saloon across the street.

The doors burst open, and two men stumbled out, locked in a heated brawl. Joshua recognized one as Tom Hawkins, a rancher with a hot temper. The other was a stranger.

"You cheatin' snake!" Tom swung wildly at the stranger.

Joshua hesitated, torn between intervening and continuing to the newspaper office. The decision was made for him when he caught sight of Faith stepping onto the boardwalk, drawn by the noise.

Their eyes met, and for a moment, the world seemed to stand still. Faith's expression was a mix of surprise and something causing Joshua's heart to skip a beat.

The moment was shattered by a pained cry. The stranger had gained the upper hand, pinning Tom against the hitching post. A knife appeared in the stranger's free hand.

Joshua's blood ran cold. Who was this man, and what had started the fight? As he walked toward them, ready to intervene, he caught Faith's attention once more. The determination in her gaze matched his own.

With the stranger's back to him, Joshua's hand inched toward his pistol. But before he could act, the scene before him changed in an instant. He stood rooted to the spot, his hand hovering near his holster as he watched the scene unfold before him.

Aggie Price, her graying hair pulled into a tight bun, had emerged from the Golden Griddle with surprising stealth. In her hands, she wielded a heavy wooden rolling pin like a seasoned warrior. Before the knife-wielding stranger could react, Aggie brought the improvised weapon down hard on his wrist.

The man yelped in pain, his grip on the knife loosening. Tom, seizing the opportunity, ducked and rolled away from his attacker.

"You meddlesome wench!" the stranger snarled, whirling to face Aggie.

Joshua's gut twisted. "Aggie, get back!" He began

drawing his six-shooter when he spotted Brodie rushing toward the widowed co-owner of the Golden Griddle.

"Aggie, step away," Brodie called.

Ignoring the sheriff, she stood her ground, the rolling pin raised defensively. "I don't take kindly to threats against my townspeople."

The stranger's eyes darted between Aggie, Brodie, and Joshua, clearly reassessing his situation. "This isn't over," he growled, backing away slowly.

Brodie advanced, his gun trained on the man. "I believe it is. You've got about ten seconds to get out of town before I arrest you."

As the stranger retreated, disappearing down an alley, Joshua rushed to Aggie's side. "Are you all right?"

She nodded, her breathing slightly uneven. "I'm fine. How's Tom?"

Joshua's gaze shifted to Brodie, who stood next to the stunned rancher. "The sheriff's helping him."

"Tom, you okay?" Joshua heard Brodie ask.

He rubbed a swelling jaw. "Thanks to Miss Aggie here."

She smiled modestly. "I've found a rolling pin has many uses beyond baking."

Despite the gravity of the situation, Joshua couldn't help chuckling. "Remind me never to get on your bad side, Aggie." His expression sobered as he turned back to Faith, who stood a few feet behind him. "We should talk. I'll walk you back to your office."

Chapter Twenty

The wooden floorboards creaked beneath Joshua's boots as they entered the Mystic Gazette office, the lingering excitement of the brawl still humming in their veins. The comfort of familiar surroundings wrapped around them, a stark contrast to the chaos they'd left behind on the streets of Mystic. Faith moved behind her sturdy oak desk while Joshua lowered himself into the chair across from her, his gaze never leaving her face.

The ticking of the wall clock seemed to grow louder in the silence. Faith let her gaze drift to the typewriter holding a half-written story. Joshua watched, his shoulders tensing beneath his cotton shirt. The air crackled with unspoken words and barely contained emotions.

He cleared his throat, breaking the stillness. His voice, soft yet firm, carried the weight of his next words. "Faith, I was wondering if you've given any thought to what I said last night. About my feelings for you."

She opened her mouth to respond, but the words caught in her throat. The tension in the room thickened, almost palpable in the fading evening light streaming through the office windows.

He leaned forward. "I know it might've come as a surprise, but I meant every word. I've cared for you for a long time now, and I believe it's high time I said something about it."

Her hands trembled as she smoothed her skirt, buying time as she gathered her thoughts. "Joshua, I..." she began, her voice barely above a whisper.

He held up a hand, a gentle smile playing at the corners of his mouth. "You don't have to say anything if you're not ready. I just needed you to know how I feel."

"It's not that I don't want to respond. There's just so much to consider."

"What's troubling you? You know you can talk to me about anything."

"We've been friends for so long, Joshua. What if..." She drew in a breath. "What if this changes everything?"

A soft chuckle escaped his lips, warm and reassuring. "Change isn't always a bad thing. Sometimes, it's exactly what we need."

Her lips curved into a small smile, some of the tension easing from her shoulders. "You always know what to say, don't you?"

"Not always. When it comes to you, I've had plenty of time to think about what I want to say."

The clock on the wall chimed, startling them both.

Faith glanced at it, realizing how much time had passed. "I should start working on tomorrow's edition," she said, reluctance clear in her voice.

Giving a slow nod, he rose from his chair. "Of course. I won't keep you from your work." He paused, his hand resting on the back of the chair. "You should know, I meant what I said. I care for you deeply. And I'm willin' to wait as long as you need to sort out your feelings."

"Thank you, Joshua. Your honesty means more to me than you know."

As he turned to leave, Faith called out, "Joshua?"

He paused at the door, looking back at her with hope shining in his eyes.

"I have been thinking about what you said. And I promise, I'll have an answer for you soon."

"That's all I can ask. Take all the time you need."

With a final nod, he stepped out of the office, leaving Faith alone with her thoughts and the gentle ticking of the clock.

Her gaze lingered on the door long after Joshua departed, her mind a whirlwind of conflicting emotions. Turning her attention inward, she allowed herself to confront the feelings she'd been trying to suppress.

Joshua's words had indeed been at the forefront of her mind, playing on repeat like a melody she couldn't shake. His confession of love had stirred something deep within her, a longing she'd scarcely dared to acknowledge.

She closed her eyes, inhaling deeply before releasing it in a slow breath. When she opened them again, her gaze fell on a framed photograph on her desk. It was a picture of her and Joshua at last year's Founders' Day picnic. Their easy smiles and relaxed postures spoke volumes about their friendship.

Picking up the photograph, her fingers traced the edge of the frame, her touch gentle, as if caressing a precious memory. She hadn't realized how much she'd been holding back until this moment, when the floodgates of her emotions threatened to burst open.

Taking a slow breath, she stood up and paced the length of her office, her footsteps muffled by the worn carpet.

"I love him," she admitted aloud, her voice stronger now. The words hung in the air, both terrifying and exhilarating. "I love Joshua Beckett."

A mix of joy and fear coursed through her veins as the full weight of her realization settled upon her. She loved him, had loved him for longer than she cared to admit.

Stopping at the window, she gazed out at the main street of Mystic. Her reflection stared back at her, eyes clouded with apprehension.

"What if it doesn't work out? What if we lose everything we've built?"

The thought of losing Joshua's friendship, of awkward encounters and strained conversations, made her heart constrict. Their bond had been a constant in her life for as long as she could remember. Could she risk their bond for the promise of something more?

She turned back toward the desk, her gaze once again falling on the photograph. The easy companionship it captured seemed to mock her current turmoil.

"What if it does work?" she mused, a glimmer of hope breaking through her fears. "What if this is the start of something wonderful?"

The conflicting emotions warred within her, each vying for dominance. Faith sank back into her chair, her shoulders sagging under the weight of her decision.

"I need to tell him. He deserves to know the truth, even if I'm scared."

With trembling hands, Faith reached for a piece of paper and her favorite fountain pen. She would pour her heart out in ink, giving voice to the love and fear tangled within her. Perhaps in writing, she could find the courage to face Joshua and speak her truth.

Faith didn't have to wait long. An hour after leaving, Joshua returned, determined to get an answer out of her. He found no words were necessary. The instant he sat down, Faith began pouring her heart out.

His eyes softened as he listened to Faith's confession. The weight of her words hung in the air between them.

"Faith," he began when she finished, "I understand your fears. Believe me, I've wrestled with them, too. I also believe in us. In our ability to face whatever comes our way."

Her gaze met his, searching for reassurance. "How can you be so sure, Joshua? We've been friends for so long. What if... what if we lose that?"

Joshua's lips curved into a gentle smile. "Because I know you, Faith Goodell. I know your strength, your determination. And I know myself. We've weathered storms before, haven't we?"

She nodded. A memory of one particular disagreement, which almost tore them apart, flashed through her mind. "We have," she admitted.

"Then we can weather this, too," he continued, his voice gaining confidence. "I'm not saying it'll be easy. But nothing worth having ever is."

"What about the town? The gossip?"

He couldn't stop a chuckle. "Since when has Faith Goodell, intrepid editor of the Mystic Gazette, cared about gossip?"

A reluctant smile tugged at Faith's lips. "Fair point."

"I'd rather face their whispers with you by my side than wonder what might have been."

Her heart skipped a beat at his words. She took a deep breath, steeling herself. "All right, let's talk about this. What are your expectations?"

He rubbed his chin, his expression thoughtful. "Honestly? I want to court you properly, Faith. To show you, and everyone else, how much you mean to me. But I also want us to take it slow, to give ourselves time to adjust to being a couple."

"I'd like that, too. I don't want to rush into anything."

"And we won't," he assured her. "We've got all the
time in the world."

As they continued to talk, their fears and hopes
laid bare, the tension in the room gradually eased.
Faith found herself relaxing, her earlier apprehension
giving way to a cautious optimism.

"You know," she said, a hint of her usual playful-
ness creeping into her voice, "this isn't quite how I
imagined this conversation going."

Joshua raised an eyebrow, curiosity sparking in
his eyes. "Oh? And how did you imagine it?"

She felt a blush creep up her cheeks. "Well, for
one, I didn't think I'd be sitting behind my desk like
I'm conducting an interview for a story."

His laughter filled the room. "Would you prefer if
I got down on one knee and recited poetry?"

"Heavens, no." Faith giggled, the sound surprising
her. "I think we've had enough drama for one day,
don't you?"

As their laughter subsided, a comfortable silence
settled between them. She found herself studying
Joshua's face, noting the tiny crinkles at the corners
of his eyes. With a start, she realized how handsome
she found him. How had she never allowed herself to
acknowledge her attraction to him before now?

"What are you thinking?" Joshua asked.

She hesitated for a moment before answering.
"I'm scared, but I'm also excited. About us. About
what this could be."

"Me, too, Faith. Me, too."

He leaned forward. "You know what? We should celebrate this moment."

"Celebrate? How?"

"How about supper at the Golden Griddle?" A boyish grin spread across his face.

She felt a flutter in her chest, a mixture of nervousness and anticipation. "Supper sounds lovely, Josh. But... are you sure? People might talk."

He reached across the desk, his calloused hand gently covering hers. "Let them talk. I'm proud to be courting the smartest, most beautiful woman in Mystic."

A blush crept up Faith's neck, coloring her cheeks. She ducked her head, a small smile playing on her lips. "Well, when you put it that way, how can a girl refuse?"

They stepped out into the cool evening air, noting the stars already sparkling against a dark midnight sky. As they walked side by side along the boardwalk, Faith couldn't help noticing the subtle change in their dynamic. Joshua walked a little closer, taking her hand and slipping it through his arm, sending shivers down her spine.

The Golden Griddle came into view, its windows glowing with warm, inviting light. The scent of homecooked meals wafted out onto the street, making Faith's stomach growl in anticipation.

"Hungry?" Joshua's eyes danced with amusement.

She laughed, the sound light and carefree. "Starving, actually."

Entering the restaurant, the bustling atmosphere enveloped them. The clinking of cutlery against plates, the low hum of conversation, and the occasional burst of laughter created a lively backdrop.

As they settled at a small table, Faith couldn't help but marvel at how different everything felt. The same worn wooden table, the same menu, the same view of the street through the window. And yet the world seemed somehow brighter, more vivid.

"What are you thinking?" Joshua asked.

"I'm thinking, I'm glad we're here. Together."

"Me, too, Faith. There's nowhere else I'd rather be."

Chapter Twenty-One

A heartbeat passed, then two, before Joshua stretched his hand across the table. His calloused fingers found Faith's, entwining them with a gentleness that belied his strength.

Her heart thundered against her ribs. This simple gesture, so public and yet so intimate, sent a thrill through her entire being. She glanced around, keenly aware of the other patrons' curious looks.

Faye Byrne leaned over to whisper something in her husband's ear, her eyes never leaving Joshua and Faith's joined hands. At a nearby table, the town barber, Elmer Moss, nudged his wife, pointing in their direction.

"Josh," Faith whispered, her cheeks flushing. "Everyone's staring."

His thumb traced a soothing pattern on the back of her hand. "Let them. I want everyone to know how I feel about you. No more hiding, no more wondering. You're the woman I love, and I'm proud to show it."

"But what will they say? The town gossips will spread the word about us being here together."

"They can say what they like. We've known each other since we were kids, Faith. They've probably been expecting this for years."

A soft chuckle escaped her lips. "I suppose you're right. It's all so new. Wonderful, but new."

"I know. But I want to do this right. No sneaking around, no secrets. You deserve to be courted properly."

As if on cue, Aggie appeared at their table, a knowing grin on her face. "Well, now, what can I get for Mystic's newest couple?"

Faith felt her face flush, but Joshua's presence grounded her. He squeezed her hand gently before addressing Aggie. "Two of your finest steaks, please. We're celebrating tonight."

Her eyes twinkled. "Celebrating, eh? About time, if you ask me. I'll have those right out for you."

After she bustled away, Faith leaned in closer to Joshua. "You really meant it when you said you wanted everyone to know, didn't you?"

He nodded, his expression earnest. "I did. I've loved you for so long. Now that I can finally show it, I don't want to waste another moment."

"I love you, too, Josh," she whispered, her voice thick with emotion. "And I'm grateful for your courage."

Sitting there, hands joined across the table, Faith felt a sense of rightness settle over her. The whispers and stares faded into the background, insignificant in the face of the love she shared with Joshua.

As the evening progressed, the initial flurry of whispers and glances from the other patrons subsided, replaced by the comfortable hum of conversation. Faith and Joshua found themselves settling into an easy rhythm, their words flowing as freely as the Moon River running through their beloved Mystic Valley.

"Do you remember," he began, his eyes twinkling with mirth, "the time we snuck into old man Morris's orchard?"

Her laughter rang out, clear and melodious. "How could I forget? You got stuck in one of his apple trees, and I had to talk Mr. Morris out of hauling you to the jail."

"I still maintain those were the best apples I've ever tasted."

"Only because they were forbidden," she teased.

Continuing to share stories and laughter, Faith marveled at how natural it felt. This was Joshua, her childhood friend, the man who'd always been there. Yet now, there was a new undercurrent to their interactions, a spark she'd never felt before.

"You know," Joshua said. "I've always admired how you took over the Gazette after your father passed. Not many women would've had the courage to tackle something so significant."

Her expression softened. "It wasn't easy. There were plenty of folks who thought a woman had no business running a newspaper."

His hand found hers again. "You proved them

wrong. You're making your mark on this town. It's one of the things I love most about you."

The warmth of his words wrapped around her like a comforting blanket. As they finished their meals, Faith felt the bond between them growing stronger with each passing moment, their shared history intertwining with the promise of a shared future.

When they finally stepped out of the Golden Griddle, the night air greeted them with a crisp embrace. He offered his arm, and Faith took it without hesitation. Walking toward her home, she felt a sense of belonging missing since her father died.

"It's a beautiful night," she murmured, her gaze drawn to the star-studded sky above.

"It is. On nights like these, I'm reminded of why I love Mystic so much. The vastness of the sky, the quiet of the town. It's as if the entire world is laid out before us."

A small smile curved her mouth. "I know what you mean. I've always believed there was something special about this place."

"I've been thinking," Joshua said. "Grayson has been talking about expanding the ranch's operations. Maybe branching out into horse breeding. He asked me if I'd be willing to take it on. Working as a wrangler does appeal to me."

Her eyes lit up. "What a wonderful idea. You've always been good at breaking and training horses."

"I was hoping you'd say that. Your opinion means a lot to me, Faith."

As they continued toward her house, Faith found herself filled with a sense of contentment and anticipation. The future stretched out before them, full of possibilities.

The soft crunch of gravel beneath his boots slowed as they approached her doorstep. The familiar, white-painted porch, illuminated by the warm glow of the lantern Faith had left burning, seemed different tonight. More significant.

Joshua paused at the front door, his gaze meeting hers with such intensity her breath caught.

"Faith," he said softly, his voice barely above a whisper. "Tonight has meant a great deal to me."

"It's meant a lot to me, too, Josh."

Joshua took a step closer, his hands resting on her shoulders. "I've been thinking about this moment for so long," he admitted, his gaze never leaving hers. "About us."

Faith felt the world around them fade away. The chirping of crickets, the distant laughter from the Starlight Saloon, and the gentle rustling of leaves in the night breeze disappeared into the background. All she could focus on was Joshua, the man she'd known since childhood, now standing before her as something more.

"Josh, I—" she began, but words failed her. How could she express the tumult of emotions surging through her? The excitement, the fear, the overwhelming sense of rightness?

Joshua seemed to understand. Slowly, giving her every chance to pull away, he raised his hand to cup her cheek. His touch was gentle, calloused fingers rough against her skin, yet infinitely tender.

"May I kiss you?" he asked, his voice husky with emotion.

"Yes, please," she breathed, barely audible.

Joshua leaned in, closing the distance between them. His lips met hers, soft and hesitant at first, then with growing confidence. Faith's eyes fluttered closed as she leaned into the kiss, her hands coming to rest on his broad shoulders.

It was everything she'd imagined and more. Sweet, tender, and filled with promise. When he lifted his head, both slightly breathless, she found herself gazing into his eyes, seeing a reflection of her own joy and hope.

A smile tilted his lips. "I think this is the beginning of something wonderful."

"I think you're right. A new chapter for both of us."

Standing there, hands intertwined, Faith felt a sense of peace settle over her.

Reaching for the doorknob, a sudden chill ran down her spine. The hairs on the back of her neck stood up, and she froze, her hand hovering inches from the brass handle.

Joshua noticed her hesitation. "What's wrong?"

She tried to dismiss the feeling. "I'm not sure. It's probably nothing, but—"

Her words were cut short by the sound of shattering glass from inside her home. Her eyes widened in alarm, meeting Joshua's now-alert gaze.

"Stay behind me," he whispered as he gently nudged Faith aside.

Heart pounding, she whispered back, "We should get the sheriff."

"You go. I don't want whoever's inside to get away."

As he turned the handle, Faith hesitated. Who could be in her home? What did they want? The *Mystic Gazette* had been stirring up controversy lately with the formation of the Women's Alliance. Could this be related?

The door creaked open, and Joshua stepped inside, then turned to Faith. "Get Brodie."

The look on his face spurred her to action. Hurrying down the steps to the street, she ran toward the house behind the jail.

Joshua let out a relieved sigh as he took another step into the house. The interior was dark, save for a sliver of moonlight streaming through a window. As his eyes adjusted, he saw nothing amiss.

"Show yourself," he called out.

A rustling sound came from the direction of Faith's study. He moved toward it, his steps cautious.

A figure darted out from the shadows, knocking Joshua off balance. The intruder barreled past Joshua, shoving him roughly against the wall.

Recovering, he rushed out of the house, his longer strides eating up the distance between him and the fleeing figure. Bursting onto the moonlit street, Joshua caught a glimpse of the intruder's face. His blood ran cold as recognition dawned.

Questions assailed him as he continued his chase. The figure disappeared around a corner, with Joshua close behind.

The sound of boots pounding the dirt echoed through the quiet side street as Joshua Beckett pursued the intruder. The familiar weight of his six-shooter nestled comfortably in his palm. He raised it, his gaze locked on the fleeing figure ahead.

"Hold it right there!" Joshua's normally soft-spoken voice boomed with unexpected authority. "Stop now, or I'll be forced to shoot!"

The intruder's pace faltered for a moment, and Joshua seized the opportunity to close the distance between them. His finger rested lightly on the trigger, ready but restrained. Joshua had never relished violence, always preferring to be the peacemaker, but he knew when force was necessary.

As he drew nearer, Joshua's mind whirled with questions. Who was this man? Why had he been in Faith's house? The thought of her in danger stirred something fierce within him.

"I won't ask again," he called out. When the man continued running, he shouted a second time.

"Last chance," Joshua warned, his voice carrying a hint of steel he knew would have surprised those who knew him as the quiet Beckett brother. "Stop now, or I'll be forced to shoot."

The weight of the moment pressed down on him. He'd always been the one to defuse tense situations, to find the peaceful solution. With the safety of Faith at stake, he found himself ready to embrace a different role.

The intruder stumbled, his body tensing as Joshua's words registered. A moment of hesitation hung in the air, before the man moved toward his holster.

Joshua's grip on his six-shooter tightened. "Throw the gun to the ground."

With a grunt of frustration, the intruder pulled out his revolver and tossed it to the ground.

"Turn around," Joshua commanded.

As the man pivoted, Joshua's eyes flickered in recognition. It was the same fellow who'd been in the fight with Tom Hawkins hours earlier.

"What in tarnation were you doing in Faith's house?"

The man's eyes darted around, searching for an escape. "It's none of your business."

Joshua's jaw clenched. "Oh, I'm making it my business."

The tense standoff was interrupted by the sound of confident footsteps approaching. Sheriff Brodie Gaines strode onto the scene. He took in the situation with a practiced sweep.

"This the man Faith said was in her house?" Brodie asked.

Joshua kept his gun trained on the intruder but nodded respectfully to the sheriff. "He is. He's also the man who was in the fight with Hawkins today."

Brodie's brows arched, the only indication of his surprise. He turned to the intruder, his tone brooking no argument. "Your name?"

The man shifted uneasily but didn't answer.

Brodie stepped closer, his face inches from the man. "Your name, now."

"Jim... Jim Rounder," he muttered.

As Brodie opened his mouth to continue his questioning, a familiar figure appeared at the edge of Joshua's vision. Faith walked toward them, her eyes intent on the scene before her.

"Is this the man who was in my house?" Faith asked, sensing the tension in the air.

Joshua felt a surge of protectiveness as Faith stopped beside him. He admired her courage, the way she didn't shy away from tough situations. It was one of the many things he loved about her, though he'd never found the right words to tell her so.

"It is," Joshua answered.

Brodie's voice cut through the moment, sharp and focused. "Mr. Rounder, care to explain what business you had in Miss Goodell's house?"

Rounder's eyes darted between the three of them, clearly searching for a way out of his predicament.

Joshua stepped forward, his patience wearing thin. "Out with it, Rounder."

The tension in the air was palpable as they waited for the man's response.

Chapter Twenty-Two

When Rounder refused to provide his reason for breaking into Faith's house, Brodie turned him around and grasped the man's wrists. The metallic click of handcuffs echoed in the tense silence.

"All right, let's go," Brodie commanded. He gripped the man's arm, steering him toward the jail.

As they walked, Joshua noticed the intruder's head swiveling from one side to the other. Was he searching for an escape route, or were others hiding in the dark to help him?

Faith stepped closer to Joshua, her fingers brushing against his arm. "Do you think he'll talk?"

Joshua shook his head slightly. "I don't know. If anyone can get him to talk, it's Brodie."

The jail loomed before them, its weathered wooden exterior a stark reminder of Mystic's early frontier roots. Brodie shoved Rounder through the door.

"Sit," Brodie ordered, gesturing to a chair in front of the desk.

Rounder complied, his posture rigid with defiance. Brodie loomed over him, his eyes hard as flint.

"Now," Brodie began, his voice carrying the weight of his authority, "you're going to tell me exactly what you were doing in Miss Goodell's house."

The man's gaze flicked between Brodie, Joshua, and Faith, who stood watching from near the door. The air in the small room felt thick with tension and unspoken questions.

A bead of sweat rolled down Rounder's temple, but he remained silent.

Brodie leaned in closer, his voice dropping to a dangerous whisper. "You broke into a home. You're looking at serious charges. Start talking, and maybe we can work something out."

Joshua watched the exchange, his hand moving to rest on Faith's shoulder. He could feel the tension in her body, knew she was itching to ask her own questions.

"Brodie," Joshua said. "Maybe we should—"

Before he could finish, Rounder's resolve cracked. "All right," he said, his voice strained. "I'll tell you what I know."

His gaze darted around the room, his fingers drumming an erratic rhythm on his thigh. He licked his lips, hesitating for several seconds.

"I followed the woman and man from the Golden Griddle." He nodded toward Joshua and Faith. "Snuck in through the back door when they were on the porch."

"Why?" Brodie pressed. "What were you after?"

Rounder's gaze locked onto Joshua. "It's not what," he said. "It's who."

"Explain," Brodie demanded.

Rounder released a long breath. "I'm looking for Cody Burke." His words hung heavy in the air. "He's a bounty hunter."

Silence fell over the room. Joshua felt as if the wind had been knocked out of him. Faith gasped beside him, her hand flying to her mouth.

Brodie's expression remained impassive, but Joshua could see the surprise in his eyes. "Are you sure his name is Cody Burke?"

Rounder shrugged. "That's what he called himself when I knew him."

"What's Burke look like?" Joshua asked.

"Big guy, over six feet. Blue eyes that see right through a man. Brownish red hair."

"Auburn?" Brodie asked.

Rounder nodded. "Yeah, auburn. I was told he had a ranch around these parts."

Brodie's jaw twitched. He glanced at Joshua before returning his attention to the prisoner. "And what business do you have with him?"

Rounder's lips curled into a bitter smile. "That's between me and him," he said, a challenge in his voice. "But I aim to find him, one way or another."

Joshua's mind whirled with questions. The man had to be talking about his brother. Cody had mentioned he sometimes used a different name when hunting outlaws. Why was Rounder searching for him? And why break into Faith's house?

"You're not telling us everything," Faith interjected. "How does sneaking into my home help you find Cody?"

The man's eyes narrowed, flickering between Faith and Joshua. "I know you're the newspaper lady. Thought I might find some information about Burke."

"Information like what?" Brodie asked.

"Where to find him. No one around here knows him. At least, that's what they say."

"Why do you want to find him?" Joshua pressed.

"I already told you. I've got important business with him. Personal business."

Joshua caught Brodie's eye, motioning for the sheriff to follow him outside. Expressions grim, the two headed out to the boardwalk, Faith right behind them.

"What are you thinking?" Brodie asked.

"I'm going to ride back to the ranch and talk to Cody. If I know my brother, he's going to want to meet with Rounder."

"Joshua?" Faith tightened the cinch on the saddle of her horse. When she learned he was riding back to the ranch, she'd insisted on going with him. "What could Cody have done to bring this kind of trouble?"

He shook his head imperceptibly as he helped her up into the saddle. "I don't know. But I plan to find out." Mounting up, he reined Jupiter toward the ranch. "Let's go."

They rode next to each other in silence for the first mile before Joshua broke the silence. "I can't figure out what Rounder wants with Cody."

"Could be a lot of reasons. Revenge for putting him in prison. Or Rounder might have information to share with Cody."

"Did Rounder act as if he wanted to share anything with my brother?"

Faith chuckled. "I suppose not."

Joshua looked over at her, not quite believing she'd agreed to be courted. Faith could have any single man she wanted in Mystic. Yet here she was, riding next to him.

"How about we pick up the pace?" Before he could respond, Faith kicked her horse and took off.

Both were still laughing when they crested the hill to look out on the ranch. From their position, they could see the entire homestead. The corrals, barn, large ranch house, bunkhouse, hay storage, and building where they kept tools and extra tack. Though the partial moon didn't provide much light, it was an impressive sight.

"Do you think you could ever live out here, Faith?"

The question surprised her, and made her stomach twist. "Are you asking if I could give up the newspaper to live on the ranch?"

"Not give up the Gazette. I'd never ask you to walk away from your father's legacy."

She waited for him to say more. Instead, he

nudged Jupiter and headed down the hill toward home.

"Jim Rounder? Haven't heard his name in a while." Cody stared down into a cup of coffee. "Hoped to never hear it again."

Most of the family was still up when Joshua and Faith walked in the front door. Annalee had made coffee and sliced more of the pie left over from supper.

Joshua exchanged a glance with Faith, reaching out to thread his fingers through hers, before asking the question both wanted answered. "How do you know him?"

When Cody looked up, there was noticeable pain in his eyes. "Rounder identified Miriam's and Sophia's killers."

The room quieted at the mention of Cody's late wife and daughter.

"Rounder rode with me to where they were hiding out. Afterward, he rode back to town with me." A brittle chuckle broke from deep in his throat. "He talked the whole way back. Drove me crazy, but it kept my mind off, well... everything."

"He's a little crusty," Faith said.

Cody looked at her and nodded. "That, he is."

"So, why do you think he wants to see you now?" Grayson asked.

He shook his head. "I have no idea. It's been a while since what happened. Maybe he's come to collect on the debt I owe him."

"Debt?" Annalee asked.

"Rounder refused payment for helping me find the killers. Instead, he asked for a chit to collect on when needed. He's probably in trouble and hopes I can help him." Cody picked up his empty coffee cup and stood. "I won't know until the two of us talk."

Cody pulled out a chair in front of Brodie's desk the next morning, then changed his mind about sitting. He wanted to get this over, discover what the erstwhile outlaw had to say.

Brodie sat on the other side of the desk, watching the man who'd been his closest friend since they were children.

Back then, they'd made a rivalry of everything. Finishing assignments, having the better lunch, racing their horses, even liking the same girl. When Brodie had told Cody he was going to marry his friend's sister one day, it had led to a fight, ending with both of them being tossed out of school for a week. Brodie still had feelings for Annalee, but he'd kept those thoughts to himself since Cody's return to Mystic.

Standing, Brodie grabbed the ring of keys, picking out the one to Rounder's cell. "Let's get this done," he said, heading to the back of the jail.

Rounder's eyes widened and a smile appeared at the sight of Cody. "If it isn't the bounty hunter. How ya doing, Burke?"

Cody stared through the bars at the man he'd let ride away in exchange for guiding him to the killers he'd been tracking. "The correct question is, what do you want, Rounder?"

Rising from where he sat on the cot, Rounder stepped toward the cell door. "Got some news for you. Get me out of here and I'll tell you."

Cody smirked. "Tell me, then I'll talk to the sheriff about letting you go. Of course, Faith will have to drop the charges for breaking into her house."

"After all I did for you? I expected a little more gratitude."

Cody let out a breath, knowing Rounder was right. He looked at Brodie. "What do you say?"

Shrugging, he unlocked the cell. "You try anything at all, Rounder, and I'll make sure you stay behind bars for longer than you can imagine."

When Rounder came through the open cell door, Brodie grabbed his arm and secured one end of the handcuffs he'd been holding to the man's wrist. Walking him to the front, he waited until Rounder sat down before securing the other end of the cuffs to the chair.

Brodie shot a look at Cody. "He's all yours." Walking around the desk, he took a seat.

Cody leaned a hip against Brodie's desk, crossing his arms. "What do you have for me?"

"First, you need to promise no matter what I tell you, I'll be let go."

"Depends on what you tell me," Cody said. "And it'll be up to the sheriff, not me."

Rounder's features drew into a tense expression, his gaze narrowing as he stared at the cuffs securing him to the chair. Raising his head, he flicked a look at Brodie before nodding.

"I know where you can find the gang who robbed the bank."

Brodie sat up straighter. "How do you know where they're hiding?"

"'Cause I rode with them."

"You were part of the gang?" Brodie asked.

"I was part of it. Not any longer. I'll tell you, then you help me get work around here, and drop any charges against me."

"I'll have to talk to the president of the bank and to Miss Goodell," Brodie said.

Rounder thought for moment, then nodded.

"So, where are they?" Cody asked.

"They're at a hotel in Bozeman. The plan is to board a train tomorrow to Seattle."

Chapter Twenty-Three

Joshua and Faith emerged from the sheriff's office after learning what Rounder had confessed. Both were relieved Brodie had learned the location of the outlaw gang and would be sending a telegram to Sheriff Foster in Bozeman.

"You did the right thing, dropping the charges against him," Joshua said as they walked along the boardwalk.

"The information about the bank robbers was more important than a broken teapot." She chuckled. "It'll be interesting to see who Brodie finds to hire Rounder."

Joshua nodded, his brow furrowed. "Seems Cody met his share of odd characters while gone from the ranch," he mused. "Makes me want to hear more of his stories. He's a different man now than he was before leaving the ranch."

"People change, Joshua. Grief can do that to a person."

"I know." He sighed. "I sure do miss the old Cody."

"Give him time. He hasn't been back very long."

A clatter of hooves drew their attention as Annalee Beckett came riding up, her light brown hair windswept from the ride. She dismounted with practiced ease, tying her horse to the hitching post.

"Do you know what happened? Is Cody all right?"

Joshua exchanged a quick glance with Faith before responding. "Rounder told Cody and Brodie where the bank robbers are hanging out in Bozeman. He's going to contact Sheriff Foster."

Annalee looked over her should at the jail. "That's good news. Is Brodie still in the office?"

"He is," Joshua said, recognizing the look of longing on his sister's face. "Why don't you stop in to let him know you're in town?"

She shook her head. "I wouldn't want to bother him."

"I doubt you could ever bother him," Faith said, empathy in her voice. She looked at Joshua. "It's time I returned to the newspaper office."

"I'll walk with you," Joshua said. "Are you heading back to the ranch, Annie?"

"Knowing Cody is all right, there's no reason to stay in town."

Faith rested a hand on Annalee's arm, lowering her voice. "You need to tell him how you feel."

"Who?"

"Who, indeed. Brodie, of course."

Annalee pursed her lips, taking one more glance toward the jail. "I can't."

Returning to her horse, she mounted up. "I'll see you at the ranch, Joshua."

"Be careful, Annie. Lots of strange things have been going on around here," he said.

She flashed him a reassuring smile. "Don't worry about me, big brother. I can handle myself." With that, she spurred her horse and galloped off toward Wild Spirit Ranch.

Joshua watched her go, a mix of pride and worry churning in his gut. He felt Faith's hand on his arm, a comforting presence.

"She'll be fine," Faith said softly. "Annalee's tougher than you think."

He nodded, his gaze still fixed on the horizon. "I know. With so much happening, I can't help feeling we're standing on the edge of something big." He looked at her, a smile playing on his lips.

The wood slats of the boardwalk creaked beneath Joshua's boots as he escorted Faith toward the Mystic Gazette office. Joshua's thoughts tumbled over one another as he contemplated what he wanted to do next.

They reached the newspaper office, and he held the door open for her to step inside. She moved with her usual grace to her desk, her fingers brushing over the typewriter keys.

"I should get started on the article about the bank robbers," she said, settling into her chair. "I won't run it until we learn if Sheriff Foster and his men were able to arrest the outlaws." She looked at the paper for a few seconds before her fingers moved over the keys.

Joshua lingered nearby, not quite ready to leave. "You know, your father would be proud of how you've carried on his legacy with the Gazette."

Her fingers stilled on the keys, and she looked up at him, a soft smile gracing her features. "Thank you, Joshua. That means a lot coming from you."

His heart skipped a beat at her words, and he found himself taking a step closer to her desk. "I mean it, Faith. You've got a real gift for words, and the courage to use them. It's one of the things I love about you."

She shook her head, but her smile widened. "You know flattery won't get you a discount on the Gazette, right?"

"It never occurred to me," he teased, his eyes twinkling with mischief. "Though I might be persuaded to offer a few exclusive ranch stories in exchange for some favorable press."

Her laughter filled the office, and he felt his heart swell with affection. This was what he loved about their friendship. The easy banter, shared history, and the mutual respect.

"I should let you get to work," Joshua said, taking a step back. "I'll see you soon." He hesitated, not ready to leave.

"Joshua? Are you all right?"

Instead of answering, he found himself moving around her desk. Reaching out, he took her hands in his, and gently pulled her to stand beside him.

Her brows rose in surprise, but she didn't resist.

She stood, her slender form close to his, the moment charged with unspoken emotion. "Joshua?" she whispered, her voice barely audible.

Before he could rethink his intentions, he wrapped his arms around her, lowering his head to capture her mouth with his. The world around them faded into a soft blur. The tender kiss continued, a culmination of years of friendship and unspoken feelings finding expression. Her hands trembled as they came to rest on Joshua's chest, feeling the steady beat of his heart beneath her palms.

As they parted, both slightly breathless, his eyes locked onto Faith's. A thousand unspoken words passed between them.

Joshua's hand lingered on hers for a moment longer before he turned and left the office, the door closing behind him. She stood there, her fingertips brushing her lips, still feeling the warmth of his kiss.

Joshua strode along the boardwalk with no thought to a destination. The familiar sights and sounds of Mystic faded into the background, his mind filled with thoughts of Faith and the future he now dared to imagine.

He paused, leaning against a post, his gaze scanning the street without really seeing it.

"Joshua!" a familiar voice called out. He turned to see Tripp Lassiter approaching, a friendly smile on his face. "You look like a man with a lot on his mind."

Joshua chuckled softly. "I suppose you're right, Tripp."

The Becketts and Lassiters had been friends for two generations, sharing property lines for several miles along Moon River. Tripp's keen eyes studied him for a moment. "Wouldn't have anything to do with a certain newspaper editor, would it?"

Joshua's surprise must have shown on his face, for Tripp laughed. "Josh, no one in Mystic would be surprised if you and Faith ended up together."

He shook his head. "Am I that transparent?"

"Only to those who know you," Tripp replied, his tone softening. "It's about time, if you ask me. You two have been dancing around each other for years."

"I love her, Tripp. I think I always have. I didn't want to risk losing her friendship if she didn't feel the same."

Tripp clasped him on the shoulder. "And now?"

"I'm going to ask her to marry me."

"Well, I'll be. Joshua Beckett, you've finally come to your senses."

Joshua laughed. "I suppose I have."

Parting ways, Joshua's steps were lighter, his resolve stronger. He knew with unwavering certainty Faith was the one he wanted to spend his life with. It was time to take the leap, to embrace the future he'd only dared to dream of until now.

Glancing around, he realized he was a few steps from Jennings Mercantile. He hesitated for only an instant.

The bell above the door of the town's general store jingled as Joshua stepped inside. Casper Jennings looked up from behind the counter, his balding head gleaming.

"Good morning, Joshua," Casper greeted, his thin frame straightening. "What can I do for you today?"

His gaze scanned the store, ensuring they were alone. His heart hammered against his ribs as he approached the counter.

"Casper," Joshua began, his voice low. "I'm looking for something special. An engagement ring."

Casper's eyebrows shot up, a knowing smile spreading across his face. "Is that so? Well, it's about time, young man. I was beginning to wonder if you'd ever get around to it."

Joshua felt a flush creep up his neck. "You and everyone else, it seems."

"Only to those of us who've watched you and Faith grow up together." He reached beneath the counter. "Now, let's see what we've got here."

He produced a small tray, several rings glinting in the dim light. Joshua leaned in, his gaze narrowing as he studied the array of gold bands and sparkling stones.

"I never thought I'd be doing this," Joshua admitted, his voice barely above a whisper.

"Love has a way of surprising us, doesn't it? Now, tell me, what kind of ring do you think Faith would like?"

His brow furrowed. "Something simple. Elegant, but not flashy. Faith's never been one for extravagance."

Casper nodded. "How about this one?" He pointed to a delicate gold band with a small, brilliant diamond.

Joshua shook his head. "It's beautiful, but not quite right." He was drawn to a simple gold band with a small, deep red stone. "This one," he said, pointing. "What's the stone?"

Casper nodded approvingly. "It's a garnet."

Joshua picked up the ring, turning it in his fingers. He could almost see it on Faith's hand, imagined her eyes lighting up as he slipped it onto her finger. "It's perfect," he breathed.

As Casper wrapped up the ring, Joshua's thoughts were a tangle of ideas. How would he propose? When?

Paying for the ring, he took the wrapped gift from Casper. The feel of the small box in his pocket seemed to anchor him to the future he was choosing.

"I wish you all the happiness in the world, Joshua," Casper said. "You and Faith deserve it."

"Thank you, Casper. For everything."

His footsteps rang on the wooden boardwalk as he made his way back to the newspaper office, the weight of the ring box in his pocket a constant reminder of his mission.

Approaching the Gazette office, he paused, taking a deep breath. Through the window, he could see Faith bent over her desk. The sight of her confirmed his decision not to put off his proposal any longer.

With a gentle push, he opened the door, the bell

above it chiming softly. Faith looked up, her eyes widening in surprise.

"Joshua? I wasn't expecting you back so soon. Is everything all right?"

He stepped inside, closing the door behind him. "Everything's fine, Faith. Better than fine." His voice was soft, but there was an undercurrent of excitement he couldn't quite hide.

She stood, her brow furrowing as she studied his face. "What's going on?"

He moved closer, his eyes never leaving hers. "I've been doing some thinking," he began, his hand moving to touch the ring box in his pocket. "About us. About the future."

Her breath caught, a flicker of hope crossing her features. "Oh?" she managed, her voice barely above a whisper.

"I realized something today. Life's too short to wait for the perfect moment. Sometimes, you have to make the moment perfect yourself."

He took another step forward, close enough now he could see the faint freckles dusting Faith's nose, the flecks of gold in her green eyes. He reached her desk in three long strides, gently taking her hands in his.

"Faith, I've known you since we were children, and in all that time, I've never met anyone who matches your spirit, your kindness, or your strength."

Her breath caught in her throat, her fingers tightening around his.

"You've been my friend, my confidante, and the

one person who understands me. I can't imagine spending another day without you by my side. Faith Goodell, will you marry me?"

Joshua reached into his jacket pocket, handing her the small box. Removing the top, he held out the simple gold band with its deep red garnet stone. She gasped, her eyes filling with tears as she looked from the ring to his face.

"Oh, Joshua," she whispered, her voice thick with emotion. "It's so beautiful."

Joshua's heart skipped a beat. "So, what do you say?"

Faith laughed, a joyous sound that filled the small office. "Yes! Yes, of course it's a yes!"

Without hesitation, he slipped the ring onto her finger, then pulled her close, capturing her lips in a tender kiss. As they parted, her cheeks were flushed, her eyes sparkling.

"I love you, Joshua Beckett. I've loved you for years, even when I thought you'd never see me as more than a friend."

"I may have been a bit slow on figuring this out. But I promise to make up for lost time."

Epilogue

Three weeks later...

The church erupted in joyous applause as Joshua and Faith turned to face the congregation, their faces aglow. Joshua's face shone with a rare display of deep emotion while Faith radiated pure happiness.

"Ready, Mrs. Beckett?" Joshua whispered, his soft-spoken tone carrying a hint of playful excitement.

"Lead the way, Mr. Beckett."

As they began their journey down the aisle, Joshua was full of gratitude. He'd known Faith since childhood, but seeing her now as his wife filled him with a sense of wonder. How had he been so fortunate?

The couple moved slowly, acknowledging well-wishers with gracious nods and firm handshakes. Joshua's quiet demeanor contrasted with Faith's more outgoing nature, yet they complemented each other perfectly.

Joshua noticed his mother, Naomi, and sister,

Annalee, waiting near the church entrance. Their arms held heavy coats for him and Faith, a reminder of the brisk Montana air awaiting them outside.

As they approached the church doors, Naomi stepped forward, her petite frame belying her strength of character. Her light blue eyes, so similar to Joshua's, brimmed with unshed tears of joy.

Naomi's voice wavered as she helped Faith into her coat. "You both look so happy. It does my heart good to see it."

Joshua bent to kiss his mother's cheek. "Thank you, Ma. For everything."

Annalee, her own eyes dancing with excitement, couldn't contain herself any longer. She threw her arms around Faith.

"Finally!" Annalee exclaimed. "I've been waiting forever for you to officially become my sister!"

Faith laughed, returning the embrace. "And I couldn't ask for a better one, Annie."

Joshua watched the interaction with amusement, thinking how fortunate he was to have these strong, vibrant women in his life. As Annalee helped him into his own coat, he caught a glimpse of Brodie Gaines, the town sheriff, watching them from a distance. There was something in Brodie's gaze as he looked at Annalee that gave Joshua pause.

As they prepared to step out into the crisp air, Faith turned to Joshua, her expression serious. "Joshua, I want you to know, I've never felt more certain about anything in my life than I do about us."

He cupped her face, his calloused hands a stark

contrast to her smooth skin. "Faith, you've made me the happiest man in Montana. No, in the whole country. I promise to spend every day making sure you never regret your decision."

Naomi cleared her throat, her eyes twinkling. "As touching as this is, we've got a celebration waiting. Shall we?"

As they emerged from the church, the brisk Montana air nipped at their cheeks, a stark contrast to the warmth of the ceremony. Joshua, his heart brimming with joy, couldn't contain himself. In a swift motion, he swept Faith off her feet, her wedding dress billowing around them as he spun her in a circle.

Her laughter rang out, clear and melodious, echoing off the nearby buildings.

Joshua grinned, setting her down gently but keeping his arms around her waist. "Just the happiest day of my life, Mrs. Beckett."

Faith's cheeks, already pink from the cold, deepened in color. "I quite like the sound of that."

Making their way toward the town hall, the festive atmosphere enveloped them. The streets were alive with celebration, the air filled with the crisp scent of autumn.

It seemed all of Mystic had gathered in the town hall. Tables groaned under the weight of a veritable feast. Golden-crusted pies cooled next to cakes dusted with sugar, while pots of hot coffee and warm cider stood ready to ward off the chill.

Standing there, holding hands, the sounds of the celebration faded into the background. For a moment, it was just the two of them. Joshua and Faith, no longer just childhood friends, but partners in life, ready to face whatever the frontier might throw their way.

Across the room, Sheriff Brodie Gaines stood near the punch bowl, his eyes fixed on the scene before him. His gaze, however, kept drifting to Annalee Beckett, who was busy slicing pieces of pie at a nearby table.

His broad shoulders tensed as he wrestled with his thoughts. *Annalee's not just Cody's little sister anymore*, he mused, watching her graceful movements. Her easy smile as she chatted with townsfolk made his heart skip a beat.

He took a step forward, then hesitated. Brodie's hand unconsciously moved to his badge, a nervous habit he'd developed over the years.

Annalee turned, catching his eye. She waved, her eyes filled with mischief. "Hey, Sheriff. You planning on guarding the punch bowl all day?"

He felt his face flush. "Just making sure no one spikes it," he called back, trying to keep his voice from shaking.

Annalee laughed. "Well, come over here and make yourself useful. These pies won't slice themselves."

As he made his way over, his heart pounding, he couldn't help but marvel at how Annalee had grown into such a capable, vivacious woman. Gone was the pigtailed girl who used to trail after him and her brothers. In her place stood a woman who could hold her own on the ranch and in town.

"I, uh, I'm not sure I'll do the pies justice," Brodie admitted as he reached her side.

She grinned up at him. "Oh, come on, Brodie. I've seen you wrangle outlaws. Surely, you can handle a few tins of pie."

As they worked side by side, Brodie found himself relaxing. The easy banter between them felt natural, yet charged with an undercurrent of something more. He stole glances at her, admiring her deft hands as she cut large pieces of cake.

Maybe it's time to stop seeing her as just Cody's little sister. Maybe it's time to see her for who she really is, he thought to himself, a glimmer of hope kindling in his chest.

Annalee's gaze swept across the crowd, her natural charm drawing others into her orbit. She caught sight of her brother, Nathan, struggling with a heavy punch bowl and excused herself.

"Nate! Hold on, I'm coming to help," she called out, hitching up her skirts as she hurried over. Without hesitation, she grabbed one side of the bowl, matching her brother's strength.

In a quiet corner of the celebration, Joshua and Faith found a moment of respite. Joshua's gaze met Faith's, a shared look of wonder passing between them.

"I can scarcely believe any of this," he said, nodding toward the groupings of family and friends.

"It's been quite a journey, hasn't it, Josh?"

He nodded. "From chasing you around the schoolyard to chasing you down the aisle. Who would've thought?"

Faith laughed, the sound warm and full of joy. "I seem to recall it was you who needed the chasing. You were always so quiet, so serious. It took me years to get you to notice me as more than just Annalee's friend."

"Oh, I noticed you," he admitted, a hint of a blush coloring his cheeks. "I was just too shy to do anything about it. If it weren't for that day at Diamond Canyon…"

Her eyes softened at the memory. "When my horse threw a shoe and you came riding to my rescue? I remember. You were so gallant, offering me a ride back to town on Jupiter."

"And you were so stubborn, insisting you could walk. That was when I knew you were something special. A woman who could hold her own, yet wasn't afraid to accept help when she needed it."

Faith squeezed his hand. "We've come a long way since then. The ranch, the newspaper, all the challenges we've faced. But I wouldn't change a thing, Joshua. Not if it led us here."

Joshua pulled her close, his strong arms encircling her slender frame. "Nor would I, Faith. Nor would I."

The lively strains of a fiddle filled the air, and Joshua's eyes lit up with excitement. "Shall we dance, Mrs. Beckett?" He offered his hand to Faith with a playful bow.

"I thought you'd never ask, Mr. Beckett." She took his hand, allowing him to lead her to the makeshift dance floor.

Across the room, Brodie Gaines stood rooted to the spot where he'd been slicing pie, his eyes fixed on Annalee Beckett. Her laughter echoed in his ears. He'd known her for years, watched her grow from a spirited girl into a capable, beautiful woman. Tonight, something was different.

Brodie's heart pounded in his chest as he took a tentative step forward. Then another. His palms were sweaty, and he wiped them nervously on his trousers.

"Come on, Gaines," he muttered to himself. "It's just a dance."

And that was the problem, wasn't it? She wasn't just Annalee anymore. She was Annalee, the woman who'd captured his heart without even trying.

As he approached, Annalee turned, her eyes widening in surprise. A welcoming smile spread across her face, causing Brodie's breath to catch in his throat.

Brodie cleared his throat, willing his voice not to crack. "Annalee. I was wondering... that is, if you're not otherwise engaged... would you care to dance?"

Annalee's smile grew even brighter. "I would love to dance with you."

Placing her hand in his, Brodie felt a surge of energy run through him. He led her onto the dance floor, acutely aware of her presence, the warmth of her hand in his, the scent of lavender surrounding her.

As they danced, Brodie found himself relaxing, drawn into the easy rhythm of their conversation.

Annalee's wit and charm had always captivated him. Tonight, as they moved together, he felt something shift.

When the music began to wind down, and the laughter of others faded away, Brodie knew he'd look back on this night as the best in his entire life.

Thank you for reading **Heart of Mystic Valley**, book two in the **Montana Becketts ♦ Wild Spirit Ranch** historical western romance series.

The series prequel, Montana Bound Marshal, is available for free on My Webstore at **https:// shirleendavies.com/product/montana- bound-marshal/**

If you enjoyed Heart of Mystic Valley, here is another series you'll want to read: **Redemption Mountain**, a historical western romance series set in the turbulent era after the Civil War.

If you want to keep current on all my preorders, new releases, and other happenings, sign up for my Newsletter at **https://shirleendavies.com/ shirleens-shop/**.

A Note from Shirleen

Thank you for taking the time to read **Heart of Mystic Valley**!

If you enjoyed it, please consider telling your friends or posting a short review. Word of mouth is an author's best friend and is much appreciated.

I care about quality, so if you find something in error, please contact me via email at **shirleen@shirleendavies.com**

Books by Shirleen Davies

Contemporary Western Romance Series

Macklins of Whiskey Bend

Thorn
Del
Boone
Kell
Zane

Cowboys of Whistle Rock Ranch

The Cowboy's Road Home, Book One
The Cowboy's False Start, Book Two
The Cowboy's Second Chance Family, Book Three
The Cowboy's Final Ride, Book Four
The Cowboy's Surprise Reunion, Book Five
The Cowboy's Counterfeit Fiancée, Book Six
The Cowboy's Ultimate Challenge, Book Seven
The Cowboy's Simple Solution, Book Eight
The Cowboy's Broken Dream, Book Nine
The Cowboy's Leap of Faith, Book Ten
A Cowboy Christmas at Whistle Rock Ranch, Book
Eleven
The Cowboy's Change of Heart, Book Twelve, Coming
Next in the Series!

MacLarens of Fire Mountain

Second Summer, Book One
Hard Landing, Book Two
One More Day, Book Three
All Your Nights, Book Four
Always Love You, Book Five
Hearts Don't Lie, Book Six
No Getting Over You, Book Seven
'Til the Sun Comes Up, Book Eight
Foolish Heart, Book Nine

Historical Western Romance Series

Redemption Mountain

Redemption's Edge, Book One
Wildfire Creek, Book Two
Sunrise Ridge, Book Three
Dixie Moon, Book Four
Survivor Pass, Book Five
Promise Trail, Book Six
Deep River, Book Seven
Courage Canyon, Book Eight
Forsaken Falls, Book Nine
Solitude Gorge, Book Ten
Rogue Rapids, Book Eleven
Angel Peak, Book Twelve
Restless Wind, Book Thirteen
Storm Summit, Book Fourteen

Mystery Mesa, Book Fifteen
Thunder Valley, Book Sixteen
A Very Splendor Christmas, Holiday Novella, Book
Seventeen
Paradise Point, Book Eighteen
Silent Sunset, Book Nineteen
Rocky Basin, Book Twenty
Captive Dawn, Book Twenty-One
Whisper Lake, Another Very Splendor Christmas,
Book Twenty-Two
Mustang Meadow, Book Twenty-Three
Solitary Glen, Book Twenty-Four
Ghost Lagoon, Book Twenty-Five
Renegade Woods, Book Twenty-Six
A Redemption Mountain Christmas, Book Twenty-
Seven
Hidden Horizon, Book Twenty-Eight, Coming Next in
the Series!

Montana Becketts ♦ Wild Spirit Ranch

Montana Bound Marshal, Prequel
Wild Spirit Revival, Book One
Heart of Mystic Valley, Book Two
Storm in Montana, Book Three, Coming Next in the
Series!

MacLarens of Fire Mountain

Tougher than the Rest, Book One
Faster than the Rest, Book Two
Harder than the Rest, Book Three

Stronger than the Rest, Book Four
Deadlier than the Rest, Book Five
Wilder than the Rest, Book Six

MacLarens of Boundary Mountain

Colin's Quest, Book One,
Brodie's Gamble, Book Two
Quinn's Honor, Book Three
Sam's Legacy, Book Four
Heather's Choice, Book Five
Nate's Destiny, Book Six
Blaine's Wager, Book Seven
Fletcher's Pride, Book Eight
Bay's Desire, Book Nine
Cam's Hope, Book Ten

Romantic Suspense

Eternal Brethren Military Romantic Suspense

Steadfast, Book One
Shattered, Book Two
Haunted, Book Three
Untamed, Book Four
Devoted, Book Five
Faithful, Book Six
Exposed, Book Seven
Undaunted, Book Eight
Resolute, Book Nine
Unspoken, Book Ten
Defiant, Book Eleven

Peregrine Bay Romantic Suspense

Reclaiming Love, Book One
Our Kind of Love, Book Two

Find all of my books at:
www.shirleendavies.com/books.html

About Shirleen

Shirleen Davies writes romance—historical and contemporary western romance, and romantic suspense. She grew up in Southern California, attended Oregon State University, and has degrees from San Diego State University and the University of Maryland. During the day, she provides consulting services to small and mid-sized businesses. But her real passion is writing emotionally charged stories of flawed people who find redemption through love and acceptance. She now lives with her husband in a beautiful town in northern Arizona.

I love to hear from my readers!
Send me an email: shirleen@shirleendavies.com
Visit my Website: www.shirleendavies.com
Sign up to be notified of New Releases:
www.shirleendavies.com/contact
Follow me on Amazon:
amazon.com/author/shirleendavies
Follow me on BookBub:
bookbub.com/authors/shirleen-davies

Other ways to connect with me:
Facebook Author Page:
facebook.com/shirleendaviesauthor
Pinterest: pinterest.com/shirleendavies
Instagram: instagram.com/shirleendavies_author
TikTok: shirleendavies_author
Twitter: www.twitter.com/shirleendavies

Heart of Mystic Valley is a work of fiction. Names, characters, places, and incidents are either products of the author's imagination or used fictitiously. Any resemblance to actual events, locales, or persons, living or dead, is wholly coincidental.